DW

"Why did you take that car?"

Adam's eyes blazed with anger. "You took that car because you wanted to prove something about yourself. Didn't you?" he demanded.

"Oh, really!" Toni said. "All this fuss just because I tricked a Formula One driver into letting me try out his car. I do have an international license, you know. I was only trying the thing out for size."

"Were you?" Adam said. "Or were you trying yourself out for size? You could have been killed. That's not courage, it's stupidity!"

"And just what are you so all-fired angry about, anyway?" Toni asked. "Anyone would think you were worried about me."

But of course he wasn't worried about her. All Adam York ever worried about was his own precious self....

SALLY WENTWORTH
is also the author of these

Harlequin Presents

and these

Harlequin Romances

Many of these titles are available at your local bookseller.

For a free catalogue listing all available Harlequin Romances
and Harlequin Presents, send your name and address to:

HARLEQUIN READER SERVICE,
M.P.O. Box 707, Niagara Falls, NY 14302
Canadian address: Stratford, Ontario N5A 6W2

SALLY WENTWORTH

race against love

Harlequin Books

TORONTO • LONDON • LOS ANGELES • AMSTERDAM
SYDNEY • HAMBURG • PARIS • STOCKHOLM • ATHENS • TOKYO

Harlequin Presents edition published February 1981
ISBN 0-373-10414-6

Original hardcover edition published in 1980
by Mills & Boon Limited

Copyright © 1980 by Sally Wentworth. All rights reserved.
Philippine copyright 1980. Australian copyright 1980.
Except for use in any review, the reproduction or utilization of
this work in whole or in part in any form by any electronic,
mechanical or other means, now known or hereafter invented,
including xerography, photocopying and recording, or in any
information storage or retrieval system, is forbidden without
the permission of the publisher, Harlequin Enterprises Limited,
225 Duncan Mill Road, Don Mills, Ontario, Canada M3B 1Z3.

All the characters in this book have no existence outside the
imagination of the author and have no relation whatsoever to
anyone bearing the same name or names. They are not even
distantly inspired by any individual known or unknown to the
author, and all the incidents are pure invention.

The Harlequin trademark, consisting of the word HARLEQUIN
and the portrayal of a Harlequin, is registered in the United
States Patent Office and in the Canada Trade Marks Office.

Printed in U.S.A.

CHAPTER ONE

'JUST what the hell do you think you're doing?'

Toni switched off the engine and saw that the driver of the other car was about to get out and come across to her. Darn! She hadn't the time to waste on an argument, and was definitely in too much of a hurry to drive around looking for another parking space. Her appointment was at three and it was almost that now. Which was why she had nipped into the first available space she had come to even though she had seen that another car was already about to back into it. Naughty, she knew, but she just couldn't afford to be late for this appointment; it might just mean the turning point in her whole career, her whole life! Well, she would just have to brazen her way out and get rid of the nuisance quickly, which shouldn't be too difficult—he was only a man, after all.

Opening the door of her low-slung sports car, Toni swung her long, shapely legs, clad in sheer nylons and high-heeled crocodile skin shoes, to the ground just as the irate driver came up to her. His glance swept over her and came back to the legs. Inevitably. They *were* gorgeous legs. Slowly Toni stood up and gave the man her wide, innocent look.

'Did you say something?'

She waited for him to stammer an inarticulate reply —the usual reaction of any man getting the full treatment from eyes of an unusual smoky violet colour with very thick, dark lashes, set in a finely-boned face

that was definitely up to standard. She shut the car
door, expecting him to mutter an apology and take himself off—either that or make a pass, it was always one
or the other.

But to her surprise the man did neither. If anything
his frown deepened as he gestured towards his car, an
extremely expensive-looking Rolls Corniche, which
was still in the middle of the road, its engine purring.
'As you can see, I was already about to back into this
space before you came along.'

'Oh, *were* you?' Toni added bewilderment to the
innocence. 'But I thought you were pulling away.'

But the silly man seemed quite immune.

'Well, now that you know I wasn't, would you
please be good enough to move on so that I can park?'

Toni looked at the man in growing dislike—not
that she let it show, of course, that was one of the first
rules : never let a man know what you really think of
him if you want to use him. She took a moment to
sum him up; about thirty-five, so in what was laughingly considered to be the prime of manhood, although
most men considered themselves to be in that from
twenty-five to sixty! And as he was also tall—over
six feet—broad-shouldered and reasonably good-looking in a hard, arrogant sort of way, he obviously thought
himself fully entitled to assume an I'm a man, you're
only a woman, therefore you do what I say, attitude.
Well, two could play at that game.

She changed to the helpless female look and, after
glancing up and down the street, said, 'But there aren't
any more spaces.'

An exasperated expression came into the man's dark
grey eyes. 'I'm afraid I can't help that. You'll just have
to drive along until you find one. And now, if you don't

mind, I'm in rather a hurry,' he added pointedly.

Anger flickered through her. All right then, if the idiot man wouldn't take himself off feeling that he had behaved chivalrously in giving up the parking space to a lady as she had meant him to, then he would just have to learn the hard way. With her keys in her hand she turned to the car as if to submissively obey him— but then deliberately put the key in the lock and turned it. Without waiting to see his reaction she quickly walked round behind the car and slipped the coins she had ready in her pocket into the slot of the parking meter.

'Now wait a minute . . .'

The man took a couple of angry strides towards her and reached out as if to catch hold of her arm, but Toni stepped nimbly out of reach and said, 'On the contrary, I wouldn't wait even a minute if I were you. Look!' She raised her arm to point towards where a traffic warden was walking purposefully along the pavement towards them. Then she looked at him mockingly and said, 'You really shouldn't leave your car parked in the middle of the road if you don't want a parking ticket, you know.'

He glared at Toni in impotent rage, looking very much as if he would have liked to get hold of her and shake her, but the meter maid was almost upon them now, her notebook already in her hand, and he had to hurry over to his car. And if the contemptuous look he threw her when he heard her laugh at his discomfiture was designed to wither her, then he had again mistaken her character. Toni slung her bag on her shoulder and turned to hurry towards the television company's offices quite unperturbed. Okay, it had been a rotten trick to pull, and one she would only resort to in desperation, but too many men had tried to use her in the past for her to have any compunction about turning the tables now, so she dismissed the incident from her mind and gave her attention instead to the appointment ahead of her.

She had tried to get sponsorship for various events so many times in the past that she could almost anticipate every line of the interview. Firstly she would have to get over the interviewer's initial reaction on seeing her and convince him that someone as good-looking as she really did want to pursue a career as a racing and rally driver and was asking for financial help to further that ambition. But more often than not they didn't take her seriously, thought that she was just trying to pull some sort of publicity stunt to get her name and picture in the papers. And if she did manage to get a sponsor, it was usually from the cosmetics industry or from someone who wanted to exploit her as a woman in a hitherto completely male-dominated environment— use her as a gimmick in fact. Even now, when she had won numerous big events and had a consistently good record, so that her name was becoming well-known in driving circles, she still found it hard to get the right sort of sponsorship, whereas a man in the same position could have taken his pick of offers. And that was why this interview with a director of the commercial television company, Century Vision, which was a relatively new and growing company, was so important. It would give her the right sort of coverage and make her name known to so many people that she would never be dismissed as a playgirl amateur again. And it was almost her last chance; the big international Royal Car Club Rally was due to take place in November, in just under three months' time, and if she didn't get a soon she would have to shop around for minor sponsors and try to borrow the rest of the money herself, or else withdraw her entry, which would be a big disappointment, not to mention bringing her father's wrath down upon her head. He would accuse her yet again of not trying hard enough.

Toni sighed a little bitterly, but then shook off the feeling as she ran up the steps into Century House, the towering building that comprised the company offices and studios. Only a few minutes late, thank goodness. Crossing to the reception desk, she said to the girl behind it, 'My name is Antonia Wyndham. I have an appointment with a Mr York—Adam York.'

The girl glanced at an appointment pad. 'Oh, yes, Miss Wyndham. If you'd like to take the elevator to the fifteenth floor and then turn left, you'll find Mr York's offices at the end of the corridor.'

'Thanks.'

Toni walked over to the set of elevators and pressed the button, then took a quick, clinically-analytical look at herself in a floor-to-ceiling mirror that ran the length of a nearby wall. Shoulder-length mid-brown hair, cleverly cut to look casual but neat, make-up sufficient to emphasise her eyes but not overdone, fashionable but also practical check tweed skirt with a jacket that toned with the basic deep lilac colour; an outfit that had been carefully chosen not to appear too frivolous but definitely not too masculine. That, too, was something she sometimes had to guard against—not that anyone seeing her slim, graceful figure and not knowing her occupation would ever jump to that conclusion! It was just that it was often taken for granted that any woman who wanted to get on in a man's world of necessity lost her femininity in the process—one of the more common fallacies she'd met with during the last few years.

The elevator whisked her smoothly up into the heights of the giant bulding and she walked quickly in the direction she'd been given, wondering if Bill Claydon was already there, although she knew he would be; he was always at least ten minutes early for any appointment, however trivial. Not that she really needed him; but sometimes just showing the intended sponsor that she had behind her an experienced mechanic — who was a man and therefore could be taken seriously of course — had often turned the tables in her favour when the sponsor had been undecided about using his company's money or products on her behalf. And it was true that Bill was an excellent mechanic, but he was elderly now, in his sixties, and he wasn't fast enough when a speedy repair or tire change was vital, and he had got left behind on all the the new innovations that were always coming into the sport to make it even faster and more interesting.

There were double glass doors at the end of the corridor with ADAM YORK painted on in elegant gold lettering. An equally elegant receptionist directed her to a thickly-carpeted waiting room where Toni found Bill sitting in a large comfortable-looking leather armchair reading a magazine.

'You're late,' he said accusingly as soon as she walked through the door.

Briefly she replied, 'Traffic hold-up. Has Mr York sent for us yet?'

He shook his iron-grey head, 'Waiting for you to turn up, I expect,' then went back to his magazine and ignored her.

Toni too picked up a magazine and sat down, but

she looked at Bill over the top of it. He was wearing his black suit again, the same one he had worn for all formal occasions ever since he had bought it to attend her mother's funeral nearly fifteen years ago. And he never looked at ease in it, always putting his hand up to the collar or moving his shoulders as if it was too tight for him. He was only ever really happy in a pair of oil-smeared overalls, his head under the hood of a car and a spanner in his hand as he tinkered with the engine.

The receptionist came in and gave them a professional smile. 'I'm so sorry, but Mr York has been delayed and hasn't yet returned from his lunch appointment. May I get you a cup of coffee while you're waiting?'

They both refused and when she'd gone Toni shot a glance at Bill.

'You were still late,' he growled before going back to the article he was reading.

Toni sat back with a sigh. That was the trouble with having to work with someone who had known you since early childhood, they went on treating you like one for evermore, and she had no doubt that her lateness would be reported to her father. Not that she blamed Bill, she knew he liked and cared for her in his gruff way, but he was no match for her father, who would have every detail of the interview out of him before he'd been back at the house in Surrey for two minutes. And the next time she went home for a visit she knew that her father would be waiting to point out every mistake, every lost opportunity, and tell her how he would have conducted the interview if only he'd been able to go himself. And then the savage bitterness and anger would come back into his face and Toni

would shrink inside with guilt and the terrible feeling
of helpless futility, the knowledge that she had never
pleased him, no matter how desperately she'd tried. But
if she got a sponsor for the R.C.C. Rally and managed
to win it, perhaps then—just perhaps—he might be
pleased with her at last.

It was another quarter of an hour before the receptionist again came into the room and told them that Mr
York had arrived and would see them right away. She
led them further into the office suite and showed them
into a large, well-lit room that was more like a lounge
than an office, with comfortable modern armchairs set
round a circular, glass-topped coffee table and several
very good modern paintings on the walls. The room
was empty for the moment, but Toni hardly had time
to examine the nearest of the pictures when another
door in the side of the room behind her opened and a
man said, 'I'm so sorry to keep you waiting. A parking
problem, I'm afraid. Our private car-park under this
building is being re-surfaced and is closed at the moment.'

Even before he'd finished speaking Toni was filled
with a terrible sense of foreboding and, very slowly and
reluctantly, she turned to have her fears confirmed.
She'd stolen the parking place of the man she desperately wanted to sponsor her on the rally!

As she turned towards him the look on Adam York's
face changed from one of polite apology to incredulity
and then to an expression she couldn't fathom but had
no difficulty in guessing. For a moment their glances
held and then he came further into the room.

'How do you do, Miss Wyndham. I believe we met
before—briefly.'

Toni shook his outstretched hand, glad that she was

still wearing her glove, and said rather hoarsely, 'So we did.'

He turned to shake hands with Bill then and exchange a few words with him while Toni wondered what on earth she could do to gloss over that unfortunate first encounter. An outright apology, perhaps? It would depend entirely on whether Adam York had a sense of humour and would see the funny side of it, or whether he was the type to take malicious satisfaction in getting his own back by making her smart all through the interview and then refusing his support. At the moment it was too soon to gauge his reaction, she would just have to play it by ear.

Bill settled himself in one of the armchairs and Adam York turned towards her. 'Won't you sit down, Miss Wyndham?'

Toni looked at him uncertainly, wondering if now was the time to apologise, a little frown of worry between her eyes, the words hovering on her lips. But as she watched him, Adam York's left eyebrow rose mockingly and his mouth twisted into a sardonic grin.

Toni's mouth closed tight shut. She knew where she stood now, knew that he was going to make the most of her discomfiture. Grimly she crossed to a chair beside Bill and sat down. If she had been alone she would have just walked out, but she owed it to Bill to see it through, to go through the motions even though she knew it was useless and was only prolonging the agony—besides, he would tell her father. But inside she seethed with impotent resentment, this next half hour was going to be hell!

It started normally enough, though, as Adam York said, 'Well now, I understand that you want our sponsorship for your entry in the R.C.C. Rally, but perhaps first you could tell me what you could offer us in return for our investment?'

Bill immediately opened up his briefcase and took out a portfolio. He glanced at Toni, but she motioned him to go ahead. 'First and foremost, of course, we would have your company's name painted on the car itself and as the rally would be widely covered by the media it would appear in newspapers and car magazines as well as sports programmes and newsreels. We can also offer you a basis around which you can build an advertising campaign.' Bill expanded this at some length and then went on, 'Also Toni would, of course, make herself available to you if you wanted her to make any public appearances with the car, talk about what it's like to drive competitively, that sort of thing.'

For a moment both men looked at her, Adam York still with the slightly sardonic curl to his lips, Bill somewhat bewilderedly; she had usually taken over putting their case in an interview long before this, emphasising the advantages they had to offer far more forcibly and persuasively than he could. But today she sat silently, unwilling to give their interviewer even the slightest opportunity to make some sarcastic remark at her expense before throwing them out.

When Bill finished his sales talk, Adam York offered them cigarettes from a silver box on the table and when they both refused lit one for himself and sat back in his chair, apparently quite at ease. His cold grey eyes settled on Toni and she stiffened and sat forward, her hands clasped together in her lap.

'Perhaps you would care to tell me what experience you've had, Miss Wyndham—in rally driving, that is,' he added provocatively.

Her jaw tightening, Toni snapped out, 'I've been

driving professionally for the last five years and have an International Licence—that means I'm qualified to drive in races and rallies open to comparable drivers all over the world,' she explained for his benefit, doubting if he knew anything at all about the sport. 'I've also won several championships, and my class in a great many other rallies. And I've taken part in Formula Ford 1600 races on the Continent.'

He looked at her sharply. 'That's motor-*racing*, isn't it?'

She nodded briefly. 'Yes.'

For a moment he looked at her silently, his eyes narrowed against the smoke, then he said abruptly, 'Have you ever taken part in an R.C.C. Rally before?'

Toni's head came up. 'No.' And she thought, here it comes, now he's going to use that as an excuse not to sponsor me.

But instead he said, 'The R.C.C. Rally lasts for ten days and is over some of the roughest country in Britain; what makes you think you have the strength and stamina to last out that long?' His eyes travelled down her slender figure. 'You certainly don't look as if you're tough enough to undertake such a gruelling race,' he said bluntly.

'I've had a great deal of experience; I know how to conserve my strength—and I'm also a lot tougher than I look,' Toni answered caustically, her chin up and a challenge in her eyes.

But he didn't rise to it. He merely said, 'And what would you want from us?'

Toni immediately became businesslike; she couldn't not be, even though she knew it was a waste of time. 'The car, of course, and all the modifications and accessories it will need to make it ready for the rally;

at least two service vans with experienced crews for repairs and servicing during the rally itself.' And, because she knew she wasn't going to get anything anyway, she threw in, 'Plus the fee for a really good navigator and all expenses, not only during the rally but while in practice, too.'

Beside her she heard Bill make a hastily smothered choking sound and when she looked at him saw him give her a sidelong look of agonised puzzlement. But she was past caring now and just wanted to get the whole farcical interview over with. Well, she'd given Adam York his opening; now all he had to do was to make some cutting retort about not wasting his company's money on someone who couldn't be depended on not to resort to trickery as she'd already done. Which would give her the opportunity to tell him just what she thought of his cat and mouse games, and then they could all go home.

Her belligerence must have shown in her voice and attitude, but she couldn't see his reaction because he got up and walked over to the window and stood there for a few minutes, his back to them. Tony looked at his broad outline in the well-cut dark suit exasperatedly. How much longer was this going on?

A phone on the coffee table bleeped shrilly and made her jump. Adam York murmured an apology and came to answer it.

'Yes, put him on the line. Hallo ... that was quick work. No, as a matter of fact I've already found out by other means. Thanks all the same. I appreciate it. Goodbye.'

He put down the receiver and looked at them thoughtfully. Toni's grip tightened on her bag, but she forced herself to look back at him with cold disdain.

This was one mouse who wasn't afraid of the cat!

Slowly he said, 'I've been interested in what you've told me, but naturally I can't give you an answer here and now—it will have to be discussed with the Financial Director and perhaps one or two other people in the company before any definite decision can be made. But we may be able to come up with something, and I'll let you know as soon as possible.'

Bill stood up immediately. 'That's very kind of you, Mr York,' he said heartily. 'And it was very good of you to give us so much of your time. I know you must be a busy man. Come on, Toni.' He put a hand under her elbow and pulled, rather than helped, her to her feet. Toni looked over his shoulder at Adam York, a frown of puzzlement in her eyes, but then they cleared as she realised that he intended to keep her dangling on the hook for as long as possible. The swine! Anger filled her as she foresaw how he would keep baiting her with false hopes, excuses for delaying a definite decision, playing with her until it was too late anyway.

She said goodbye curtly and allowed Bill to shepherd her through the door and down the corridor. They had got almost to the elevators before she exclaimed, 'Oh, I've left my gloves! I'll have to go back for them. You go ahead, Bill, don't bother to wait for me. I'll give you a ring tonight.'

She turned quickly and hurried back along the corridor, ignoring Bill who called after her. He made to follow her, but the elevator came just then and he looked first at her retreating back and then the elevator undecidedly, but then hastily stepped into the elevator as the doors began to close.

Toni pushed open the door of Adam York's office, not bothering to knock. He was half sitting, half leaning on the back of one of the chairs, facing the door, her gloves in his hands, passing them through his fingers and looking down at them thoughtfully. He looked up as she opened the door but betrayed no surprise, it was almost as if he had been expecting her. Slowly Toni stepped into the room and shut the door, leaning against it, her eyes never leaving his.

He held out the gloves to her. 'What would women do without gloves or an umbrella they can leave behind as an excuse to return?' he asked in amused mockery.

Moving forward, Toni reached out to take the gloves, but for a moment he wouldn't let go, his eyes watching for her reaction.

Toni looked at him malevolently. 'You're really enjoying yourself, aren't you?' she said fiercely. 'You're just the type to get sadistic pleasure out of keeping me on tenterhooks, worried in case you said anything in front of Bill. And that last bit—keeping hope alive instead of coming right out and saying that we hadn't a hope in hell of getting any backing from you—why, that was masterly. Only a super-swine would have thought of that! But then I expect you've had a lot of practice to be so good at it.'

His jaw tightened at her rudeness and for a moment she saw anger in his face again, but then he let go of the gloves and said bitingly, 'Little girls who play tricks on people should be prepared to take the consequences—whatever they may be.'

Her mouth tight, Toni said, 'I am *not* a little girl.'

His eyes ran over her again, slowly, appraisingly. 'No,' he agreed silkily, 'I see you're not.'

Eyes murderous, Toni turned on her heel and strode towards the door. As she opened it, he said calmly, 'I meant it, you know. I may be able to do something for you.'

Toni turned in the doorway and gave a brittle laugh, her eyes sparking with anger. 'You really expect me to believe that? And even if you could, I'd rather not take part in the rally than accept a penny from *you*. As far as I'm concerned you can go to hell!' And she slammed the door behind her—but not before she'd heard his mocking laughter, a sound that filled her with impotent anger whenever she thought of it.

As she expected, Bill hadn't gone home but was waiting for her downstairs in the foyer, full of querulous questions about why she'd asked for more than they'd agreed on, and worrying about what he should tell her father. Toni managed to fob him off by saying that they could always agree to take less and eventually he left her to go to the nearest Underground station, still grumbling under his breath.

Toni made her way back to her car, shutting the door thankfully and leaning her head back against the head-rest for a few moments, her eyes closed. Today just wasn't her day! Of all the men to cross swords with it had to be an arrogant, sadistic type like Adam York. She groaned aloud, but then determinedly leaned forward and started the car, shrugging off the tension of the last hour and mentally preparing herself to concentrate on the task of driving across London at one of the peak traffic hours of the day.

Knowing London as well as she did, Toni was able to take several short cuts through the back streets, but even so it took nearly an hour to reach her apartment in a quiet side street near Swiss Cottage. The sound of a lively beat number, played very loud, hit her ears as she unlocked the door and she had to shout above it. 'Carinna!

Turn it down. You'll have the neighbours complaining again!'

As she passed, she banged on the bathroom door to emphasise her point, and then went on into the tiny kitchen where she set down a bag of shopping that she had bought earlier and began to put the things away in various cupboards. The music was turned down obediently and soon Carinna came into the kitchen wearing a pink towelling bathrobe, her long blonde hair piled into an untidy knot on her head, her feet thrust into a pair of rather worn mules.

'Hi, you're home early,' Toni greeted her. 'How did the session go?'

'Okay,' Carinna answered laconically, perching herself on a stool and yawning. 'It was all studio work. They wanted to know why you weren't on the assignment, but I told them you had more important things to do today than using your legs as display stands while they photographed their new range of tights.' She looked at Toni expectantly. 'Well, how did you make out? Did you get their sponsorship?'

Toni hesitated for a moment, then said with determined offhandedness, 'No, it turned out they weren't really interested. I'm going to make a coffee, do you want one?' And she began to busy herself with getting out cups, her face averted.

'Not interested? Then why did they bother to see you?'

'Oh, just out of courtesy, I suppose—or curiosity. Anyway, it doesn't really matter, there are plenty of other companies I can approach.'

Carinna wrinkled her brow in perplexity. 'But I thought this was your big chance, that you had high hopes of them coming across with some money?' Her voice changed. 'Toni, will you please stop rattling those cups around and look at me? Now,' she added as Toni reluctantly obeyed, 'tell me what happened. What went wrong?'

Toni's face became vulnerable. 'Oh, Carinna, I made a hell of a mess of things,' she confessed, her eyes darkened to deep violet as they filled with despair. 'And I'll have to tell my father what happened, and he'll be so angry!' Her hands began to shake so that Carinna hastily grabbed the coffee jar she was holding and set it on the table.

'Here, come and sit down. You need something stronger than coffee.' She led her into the sitting room and sat her down in an armchair, then poured some whisky into a glass and handed it to her. 'Drink this. Purely medicinal, of course.'

Toni managed a weak smile and wrinkled up her nose at the strong taste, but her hands steadied a little.

Carinna knelt down beside her. 'Now, tell me all about it,' she commanded.

Slowly Toni did so, from the moment she had tricked Adam York out of his parking space until she had slammed her way out of his office.

'Wow!' Carinna sat back on her heels and gazed at her. 'If you decide to put a foot wrong you really go about it in a big way—hobnailed boots and all! Yes, my child, I'm afraid you have lost the chance of sponsorship in that direction, especially since you threw even the possibility of it back in his face!' She looked at Toni curiously. 'But what made you lose your temper like that? Your rule is never to let a man get under your skin, to keep cool in the face of the enemy.'

'I know.' Toni frowned. 'But there was just something about him. He was so—so damn sure of himself—taking delight in having me at his mercy, but in such a cold, contemptuous way. I suppose he expected me to beg his forgiveness, to grovel for his support. Well, I won't,' she said fiercely. 'Not for anything!'

Carinna stared at her in astonishment. 'I haven't seen you this upset because of a man in years. What's he like—your Adam York?'

'I told you—a cold, arrogant...'

'No, what does he look like?'

'Oh. Mid-thirties, tall and dark. Good-looking if you like the hard, disdainful type, I suppose.'

'And successful?'

'Well, he's a director of the television company and he drives a Rolls, so I suppose you could say he was successful, yes.'

'You didn't happen to find out if he's married, did you?'

Toni's mouth opened in exasperation. 'Carinna, for heaven's sake! You only have to hear about a man and you want to know his marital status.'

'Well, a girl has to look out for herself—and so should you. If you had a rich husband you wouldn't have to go round looking for sponsors all the time.'

'Humph.' Toni got to her feet and walked towards the kitchen. 'We've had all that out before. As far as I'm concerned marriage is out completely. Men are just around to be used whenever you might need one—just the same as they use us. In my book any girl who gets tied to a man just becomes an unpaid servant for life. And that's not for me, thank you very much.' She put the coffee into the cups and switched on the kettle rather belligerently.

Carinna followed her in and leant against the work-surface. 'It's a shame about your Adam York. He sounds quite a dish.'

'Are you crazy? I told you, he's a cold, sadistic swine. And stop calling him *my* Adam York. I'm just glad I'll never have to see him again, that's all.'

'Mm. But you can forgive even a swine a lot if he's also rich *and* good-looking,' Carinna returned thoughtfully, then held up her hands in mock surrender as she saw the look on Toni's face. 'Okay, okay, I won't say another word. But it does seem an awful waste.'

Carinna sat silently then, watching Toni as they waited for the kettle to boil, helpless anger growing in her as she saw her friend's shoulders sag dispiritedly again. At last she said fiercely, 'Toni, you don't have to tell your father! He doesn't have to know it was your fault. You can put the blame on the television company.'

Toni looked at her miserably. 'I have to, Carinna. You know I can't lie to him.'

'Oh, for heaven's sake!' Carinna opened her mouth to go on, but then closed it again. What was the use? She had urged Toni to stand up to her father a thousand times before, even to break away from him completely, but it had never been any good. Toni was too much under his domination ever to defy him.

After their coffee, the two girls spent an hour or so cleaning up the apartment and then prepared a meal, but Toni grew gradually more tense and on edge, waiting for the inevitable phone call from her father and nerving herself to face his recriminations. She looked repeatedly at her watch. Bill would have had plenty of time to get home by now and tell him of the interview. At eight she went into the bathroom to wash her hair ready for the next day's modelling assignment and had her head under the spray when she thought she heard the phone ring. Fingers fumbling, she hastily turned off the spray and groped for a towel, but after a moment gave a sigh of relief; Carinna hadn't called her, so it couldn't be her father.

Twenty minutes later she went into the sitting room and found Carinna curled up on the settee watching television and painting her nails, a cat-who-got-the-cream look on her face.

'Who was on the phone?' Toni asked her. 'A boyfriend?'

'No.' Carinna looked at her, plainly enjoying herself. 'As a matter of fact it was your Mr York.'

'*Adam York?*' Toni stared at her in amazement. 'Why didn't you call me?'

'It wasn't necessary. He merely left a message. And besides, I thought you might be rude to him again.'

'You might be right, at that,' Toni agreed with irony. 'What did he want?'

'He wants to meet you to discuss the sponsorship idea further.'

Toni sank down into an armchair opposite and gazed at her friend in wide-eyed astonishment. 'He said that? But I already told him I didn't want help from him any more.' Her look changed to one of suspicion. 'This isn't some kind of joke, is it?'

Carinna looked affronted. 'Would I do such a thing? No, cross my heart and hope to die; he *did* ring, he *does* want to meet you—in the bar of the London Hilton at seven tomorrow. He suggested lunch at first, but I said you were already engaged. No point in being too eager, and by meeting him in the evening you could get him to take you out to dinner if you hang it out long enough.'

'Carinna! You're incorrigible. You see men as nothing but a free meal ticket.'

'How else can I prospect for the perfect permanent meal ticket?' Carinna asked reasonably. 'If a man's too mean to take me out to dinner, I cross him off my list.' She looked across at Toni speculatively. 'Will you meet him?'

Toni frowned. 'Are you sure that's all he said—just that he wanted to discuss it further?' And when Carinna nodded, she got up and began to walk restlessly up and down the room. 'I suppose I'll have to,' she said at length. 'Though why he wants to see me again after I was so rude to him, I can't imagine.'

'I can,' her friend advised her. 'Couldn't it be that your Mr York—with the deep sexy voice that you didn't tell me about—has fallen for your face, your figure and your big, innocent eyes?'

'You're joking!' Toni exclaimed. 'I tried using sex-appeal on him when I wanted his parking space and he just wasn't interested. And it was war all the way through the interview. Why, the nearest he ever came to noticing I was a girl was when he ...' She broke off suddenly, a slight colour in her cheeks as she remembered the way his eyes had run over her just as she was leaving.

Carinna laughed delightedly. 'You see! But it's all right, you don't have to worry. I have a date myself tomorrow and I've just rung him and told him to meet me at the Hilton at seven-thirty, so I'll come along and chaperone you for half an hour.' She leaned back against the settee and added gleefully, 'I just can't wait to meet your Adam York!'

CHAPTER TWO

EARLY evening was a busy time and the massive foyer of the London Hilton was thronged with hurrying people as Toni and Carinna entered it the following evening. But even among that maelstrom of the rich and well-dressed they stood out from the crowd. Two young women, one blonde, one darker, but both tall, slender and attractive; Carinna wearing a long evening dress and cloak because she was going on to Regine's nightclub after dinner, Toni in a black suit with a pencil-slim skirt slit up to the knee and a small black pillbox hat with a veil that covered the top half of her face set on her head. The outfit made her look extremely sophisticated and had been chosen to give precisely that effect, just as the one she had worn the previous day had been designed to give the impression of a capable sportswoman with an outgoing personality. But today she didn't feel at all outgoing; having lost her temper once with Adam York she was now extremely wary and determined not to let it happen again. She intended to be completely in control of herself and the situation this evening, hence the sophisticated veneer and the veil to hide behind.

Without haste they made their way towards the bar, Toni's face a little grim as she wondered just why he wanted to see her and already wishing that she hadn't come; but at least it had placated her father's icy anger when he had rung the previous night, even if it was only for a day.

26

They paused in the entrance to the bar and a great many heads turned to look them over.

'Which one is Adam York?' Carinna hissed.

For a moment Toni couldn't see him, but then she looked over at the bar and saw him standing by it, his back towards them. She nodded in his direction. 'Over at the bar. You can see his reflection in the mirror.'

'Wowee!' Carinna used her most impressed exclamation. 'Superman, no less. And you told *that* to go to hell? You *are* crazy!' Then, 'Come on, let's go over and meet him.'

To her annoyance, Toni found that her heart had started to beat loudly in her chest as they walked across the room. Hastily she schooled her features into a frigid mask, afraid that he might notice her nervousness. As they got nearer he saw them in the huge tinted mirror behind the bar and deliberately turned to stand and watch them come to him.

When they reached him Toni said coldly, 'Mr York.'

'Miss Wyndham.' He returned the greeting enigmatically, his expression unreadable.

'This is my roommate, Miss Lyall. She's meeting a friend here shortly, so we shared a taxi,' she explained.

He turned to shake hands with Carinna. 'How do you do, Miss Lyall?'

'Oh, please, call me Carinna.' Her face broke into a mischievous smile as she added, 'Toni has told me so much about you Mr York.'

A look of amusement came into his grey eyes. 'I'm sure she has. And the name's Adam,' he added.

He ordered drinks for them and then Carinna asked him about his work, drawing him out with artless questions about the famous people he had met. Toni stood quietly by, content to let Carinna monopolise the conversation, watching to see if Adam York was taking the bait. He certainly seemed to be, the cold look had left his face and once he even laughed in amusement at one of Carinna's droll observations. But then he looked up suddenly and caught Toni watching him. For an instant their eyes held, but Toni immediately looked away, deliberately assuming a bored expression.

'That sounds absolutely fascinating,' Carinna was saying. 'But how do you meet all these people?'

'Mostly as guests on the Wayne Robertson chat show,' he explained. 'It's part of my job to choose the guests and I usually attend the party that's given for them after the show.'

Carinna was suitably impressed, gazing up at him with open admiration. 'Wow! You really get to choose who goes on the show?'

He nodded, then said, 'Perhaps you'd like to come along one evening and watch the show and attend the party afterwards? I think we've got the American film star Joel Anderson this week.' He turned to look at Toni. 'Both of you, of course.'

Toni immediately opened her mouth to refuse, but Carinna hastily interjected, 'Why, we'd love to.' She gave him the full treatment of her most brilliant smile. 'Thank you so much, Adam.' Then she added innocently, 'Will your wife be coming?'

He gave her a rather crooked smile. 'I shouldn't think so. I'm not married.'

Glaring at Carinna, Toni said stiffly, 'I have other plans for Saturday night—but *you* go by all means.'

'I can let you have another ticket if you want to bring your boy-friend along,' Adam York offered, the sardonic quirk back on his lips.

'Thank you, but I shall probably be going to visit my home at the weekend,' Toni returned coldly.

He gave a curt nod and turned back to Carinna, but her boy-friend arrived shortly after and whisked her away as soon as he saw that he might have some opposition.

When they had gone, Adam York turned to her and Toni found herself mentally bracing her shoulders. 'Shall we sit down, Miss Wyndham?' he suggested, and led the way to a quiet, dimly-lit booth tucked away in the corner.

Once there, he ordered fresh drinks and sat silently until they arrived, then picked up his glass and sat back in the booth to look at her, his eyes narrowed.

Unexpectedly he said, 'You look very different today.'

'Do I?'

'You know you do. Which is the real you, I wonder, the sophisticated fashion-plate or the practical career-woman?' He continued to look at her for a moment, but when she merely returned his look silently, her face indifferent, he abruptly set down his glass and said, 'I've talked to the other people in my company concerned and we've agreed to put a proposition to you. We're willing to give you as much backing as you need, but in return we want your co-operation in making a documentary film. Not only of the race itself but also of the build-up to it: choosing a car, getting it ready, the practice you have to put in and, in fact, all the work that goes into preparing for a big rally. We also want to do a publicity campaign to advertise the film, so we would expect you to appear in magazine-type programmes before the rally and to give as many press and media interviews as we can contrive.'

He paused to light a cigarette and looked across at her. 'You seem somewhat surprised,' he added drily.

Hastily Toni closed her mouth and blinked. 'I—I am surprised,' she admitted. 'I didn't think you'd ... that is, I ...' She bit her lip and then looked at him directly. 'Why? Why offer to do this for me after I ...' She hesitated, then said bluntly, 'After I was so rude to you yesterday?'

For a long moment he didn't answer, just sat and studied her face, as if making up his mind about something, then he looked down at his drink and said matter-of-factly, 'I'm first and foremost a television man, Miss Wyndham. And I decided that I could use you. You're a comparatively new phenomenon and will arouse more interest and curiosity among our viewers than if we did a film about a male driver. In other words you have novelty value. And by way of a bonus you are also photogenic,' he added, the way he said it making it quite plain that the remark wasn't intended as a compliment. 'So whatever my personal opinion of you and your manners, I was willing to overlook them for the sake of what could be an interesting programme.'

Toni felt her colour heighten at his rebuke and was more than grateful for the veil. 'I see,' she said stiffly.

'You haven't yet said whether you're interested in the proposition,' he reminded her.

'Of course I am. It's the chance of a lifetime. I'd be a fool to turn it down.'

'Before you finally decide I should tell you that there are two conditions to our offer.'

Toni's head came up at that. 'Conditions?'

'Yes. The first is regarding your mechanic, Bill Claydon. I'm afraid that my company insists on appointing a chief mechanic of their own choosing, some-one younger and more up to date. I'm sorry, but there it is. I know Bill Claydon will be disappointed, but we feel you will have a much greater chance of winning with a different mechanic in charge of the team.'

'Could he come along as an assistant mechanic?'

Adam York hesitated, then shook his head. 'I think he better not, don't you?'

Toni nodded, the sense of relief at not having Bill breathing down her neck mixed with feelings of guilt for being relieved at all, and compassion for Bill, who would now finally have to admit that he was too old for the game. 'Would you mind letting me have that condition in writing, please?'

He shot her a quick glance, his eyes probing. 'Of course.'

Toni sat silently for a moment, wondering how she was going to break the news. It wasn't just not having Bill in charge of the mechanical side, he was also her father's eyes and ears, keeping him informed of every-thing she did—to do with driving, that was; what she did with the rest of her life he couldn't have cared less about. She came out of her reverie to find Adam York studying her closely. Hastily she pulled herself to-gether.

'You said there were two conditions. What was the second one?'

'Ah, yes. Well, that one is rather more—er—per-sonal.'

He said it rather hesitatingly, as if—would you believe—he was unsure of his ground. Toni looked at him enquiringly, surprised that anything could shake his mammoth self-confidence. Then suddenly she real-ised just what his *personal* condition could be! Her face paled, leaving only two spots of angry colour high on her cheekbones.

Hastily she came to her feet. 'You skunk! I should have known you weren't prepared to do all that for me without expecting something in return!' Her voice became vitriolic. 'Or did you just make the whole thing up so that I'd be willing to do anything to please you? I certainly wouldn't put it past you! Well, let me tell you, Adam York, I wouldn't make myself available to you or anyone else just to take part in a race—especially *you*!' she shot at him.

Picking up her bag, Toni stepped out of the booth and went to hurry past him, but he calmly reached out an arm and caught her wrist.

'Let me go!' Toni muttered fiercely, struggling to free herself.

Adam York sat back in the booth, regarding her with a slightly disdainful look on his face, his hand clasped round her wrist as securely as a handcuff, her struggles of no avail against his hold. Then, as if the whole thing was becoming a bore, he exerted his strength and with one arm forced her back into her seat and held her there.

'Now. Perhaps we can continue our conversation from the point before you decided to act like an hysterical schoolgirl who's received her first proposition,' he said scathingly. 'And before you decide to start screaming that you're being assaulted, I'll make it quite clear that I'm not interested in making you my mistress! And I might add that I haven't yet had to resort to blackmail to get a woman I wanted!' And only then did he let her go.

Slowly Toni sat back in the seat and began to rub

her wrist, feeling her pulse throbbing wildly as she did so.

'You said it was personal,' she managed unsteadily, her eyes still suspicious.

'It is. But I merely meant that my company would not consider sponsoring you unless I come along too—as your navigator.'

'You!' Toni stared at him in appalled dismay, leaving him in no doubt, if he had any left anyway, of her opinion of him.

His mouth twisted ironically. 'Take it or leave it,' he told her evenly.

'But—but—you can't walk into an international rally just like that! It takes years of experience before a navigator becomes good enough to take part. Look,' she leaned forward to emphasise her point, 'a navigator's job is even harder than the driver's. He has to do far more background work and has to take a recce car over the known parts of the course first so that he knows every inch of the ground. And the secret stages are even harder because then he has only a short time to plot the course on the map before the stage starts—*and* he has to more or less talk the driver round the course. It's just no place for an amateur, and—well, to be perfectly honest—with you in the passenger seat we wouldn't stand a chance. We might just as well chuck the whole thing in now and save your company's money and my time.'

He heard her out, his features expressionless. 'Do you want to chuck it in?'

'No, of course I don't,' Toni answered helplessly. 'But...'

'Then you'll just have to accept me as your navigator, won't you? And I assure you that I'm not *entirely* inexperienced.'

Toni looked at him resignedly, aware that she was banging her head against a brick wall.

'Do I take it that you agree to our terms?'

She shrugged. 'What choice do I have? But I still think it's going to be a waste of time.'

'Not if you pull your weight.' He stood up. 'Let's go in to dinner and discuss the details, shall we?'

'I'm not hungry,' Toni replied in a hollow voice, wondering just what she had let herself in for.

'But I am.' He put a firm hand under her elbow and helped her to her feet. 'I've reserved a table in the restaurant here.'

When they were seated and had chosen their meal he said calmly, 'And now I think we can drop the Mr York and Miss Wyndham bit, don't you? After all, it would look rather ridiculous when we're to work so closely together.'

'All right,' Toni said reluctantly, not liking the sound of those last few words one little bit.

'Have you shared an apartment with Carinna long?' he asked conversationally as they were served with their first course.

'Nearly four years,' she answered shortly, but he raised his eyebrows enquiringly and she felt compelled to add, 'We met at a leg session and got on well together and as we were both unhappy with our digs at the time we decided to find an apartment to share.'

Adam looked at her in genuine puzzlement. 'A leg session?'

'I mean a photographic session,' Toni explained. 'We're both professional models. We both do legs, but Carinna also does hair, and I do eyes.'

He looked into her long-lashed violet eyes, made mysterious by the black lace of the half-veil. 'Yes, I can see why you might do eyes,' he observed enigmatically.

Toni changed the subject abruptly. 'When exactly do you want to make a start on this film?'

'As soon as possible. Have you a particular car in mind?'

'A Ford Escort,' Toni answered promptly. 'It would put me in the right class of entry, and they're fast and reliable.'

'Very well. The mechanic we have in mind is Steve Landors, he prepares all the cars for chases in our television plays and that sort of thing, and he has also had quite a bit of rallying experience with one of the works teams.'

Toni nodded. 'I've heard of him. He's good.'

'I'm glad you approve our choice,' Adam said with irony, leaving Toni in little doubt that it wouldn't have made any difference whether she did or not. 'I'll make arrangements for you both to go to the Ford works at Dagenham with a film crew so that you can select a car. Have you ever been on television before?'

She shook her head.

'In that case it might be useful if you came to the studios and got used to the way we work.' He glanced at her speculatively. 'Are you sure you can't make it on Saturday for the Wayne Robertson show?'

Toni hesitated, picking up her glass of wine and taking a drink to give her time to think. She didn't really have to go to visit her father on Saturday, Sunday would do just as well; she had refused simply out of perverseness because she hadn't wanted to pander to Adam York's already outsize ego. But if it was purely business....

'All right,' she agreed, 'I'll come.'

The rest of the meal was spent in Adam outlining his ideas for the documentary, which he envisaged as an hour-long film. Toni attempted to discuss what she would need for the car, but he told her rather curtly to wait until she had met Steve Landors and then tell him what she needed. Which left Toni with great forebodings about his usefulness as a navigator; if he wasn't interested in the car, then he certainly wouldn't be interested in spending his time on practice runs.

It was gone ten by the time they finished their meal and left the hotel. Adam put her into a taxi, wished her a curt 'Goodnight' and then strode quickly away, not even lifting a hand in farewell as she drove past him.

Toni sat back in her seat and sighed; what should have been one of the happiest and most exciting days in her life had somehow fallen exceedingly flat!

The tickets for the television show arrived with a brief, typewritten note telling Toni to get there early so that she could be shown round the studios first, and signed merely with the initials A.Y. in thick black ink. Such a peremptory command immediately put her back up, but she dutifully arrived at the appointed time, together with Carinna, who was determined not to miss out on anything, and was met by an extremely efficient female assistant who showed them round and explained about special make-up for colour film, outside broadcasts, pre-recording warm-ups, and so many other things that Toni became lost in the mass of technical jargon.

Eventually they were shown to their reserved front row seats and watched the 'well-known TV personality' Wayne Robertson cleverly draw out his guests in giving entertaining answers to questions they had all been

asked a thousand times before. There was the obliga-
tory rendition of his latest recording by one of the
celebrities, and then the show closed to rapturous applause by the studio audience, in which Carinna joined
wholeheartedly, her eyes sparkling at the thought of
the coming party where she would get to meet the
guests. Toni looked at her and then thought that she
must be getting cynical; even watching it live the show
had only seemed to her to be passably entertaining—
how could it be anything else when it had been running for years to the same format and had now got to
the stage of the second time around with some of the
guests!

While the rest of the audience were filing out, they
and some other invited people were conducted to a
room near the studio where all the celebrities were
gathered together with some members of the band and
executive employees of Century Vision. The girls were
given drinks and a couple of men immediately came
over and introduced themselves, but Toni didn't take
too much interest in the conversation, leaving Carinna
to do most of the talking. She was on the look-out for
Adam York, and presently saw him come into the room
with a pleasant-faced man who looked to be slightly
younger, although in height and build they were much
the same. They stopped to pick up a couple of drinks
and then Adam brought his companion directly over
to them.

As soon as they saw Adam coming towards them the
first two men melted discreetly away. Adam nodded a
greeting and said, 'I'd like you to meet Steve Landors,
your chief mechanic on the rally project. Steve, this
is Antonia Wyndham and her friend Carinna Lyall.'

They shook hands and Steve gave her a warm smile.

'I'm looking forward to working with you, Antonia. You've a good reputation as a driver, if the motoring press is anything to go by.'

Toni returned the smile, taking an immediate liking to his free and easy manner. 'Thanks, but the name's Toni.'

'Doesn't anyone call you Antonia?' Adam asked.

She shook her head. 'No, I've been Toni from the moment I was born.'

She didn't think there had been anything in her voice, she was pretty good at hiding her feelings now, after so long, but Adam gave her a sharp glance, his brows drawn together in a frown, so that she hastily turned to Steve and asked him when they were to choose the car.

'On Tuesday. If you like, I'll pick you up and we can drive down together.' He turned to Carinna and smiled. 'Are you a driver, too?'

Carinna shook her head. 'Oh no, cars aren't my scene.' Slipping an arm into Adam's, she said coaxingly, 'Let's leave them to discuss their precious rally, shall we?' Then, pouting a little when he hesitated, 'You *did* promise to introduce me to Wayne Robertson and his guests.'

Adam smiled down at her. 'So I did. Very well, let's go and see if the famous live up to your expectations.'

He led her off, Carinna clinging to his arm and laughing excitedly. Toni watched them for a few moments and then turned back to Steve, only to find that he, too, was gazing after them, but when she said his name he immediately turned and gave her his full attention.

They spent well over an hour discussing their plans for the rally and Toni found him far more knowledge-able and keen than Bill had ever been. He also inspired in her the confidence that every driver needs to have in their back-up team, the certainty that he would be where he said he would be and at the right time. She would, in fact, have been far more optimistic about her chances if it hadn't been for the one big fly in the ointment, namely Adam York as her navigator.

As she drove home that night, Carinna sitting beside her and chattering away about the celebrities, Toni tried to work out in her mind just why Adam had insisted on the condition. He had shown his opinion of her in no uncertain terms, so it wasn't *that*. Was it to make sure she was up to standard and wasn't a waste of his company's money? But any motoring expert could tell them the answer to that one—and they must surely have checked her out before they made her the offer. Which left only one other reason that Toni could think of—that it was purely from a narcissistic wish to be seen on television. Which didn't augur well for the ten days of the rally which they would have to spend in such close proximity, and which, Toni found, she wasn't looking forward to one little bit!

The following day she lingered on the drive down to Surrey, enjoying the warmth of the September morning, her eyes dazzled by the colours of the trees as the leaves turned to the bright yellow and golds of autumn. Turning off the main road, she drove through country lanes as old as the land itself, sometimes set between high banks, sometimes arched over by trees so tall that they blotted out the sky and only dappled rays of sunlight penetrated them, as quiet and mysterious as a green cathedral. The house, when she reached it, looked just the same; a beautiful Queen Anne place of red brick, mellowed by the years, but there was the same air of neglect about it as on her last visit only a few weeks ago; paint peeling off the windowsills, a driveway that needed weeding, the lawn overgrown. Not that it would take much to set it to rights, but Toni knew that her father no longer took any real interest in the place since her mother had died.

Slowly she got out of the car and walked round to the back of the house towards the great barn where she knew her father and Bill would be working. The big, heavy doors were standing wide open and she could hear the throaty roar of a high-powered engine even from some distance away. They were together at the far end of the barn, Bill leaning over the engine of the racing car, her father nearby watching him and shouting out instructions over the noise. Neither of them noticed her as she paused in the doorway; they were too engrossed in the project they had been working on for the last ten years.

Little motes of dust danced in the sunlight of the open doorway as Toni stepped through it, her shadow uneven on the concrete floor. Bill looked up, saw her and told her father. Toni watched him make the concentrated effort of lifting a finger to press a button that turned the wheelchair in which he had been a prisoner ever since the Grand Prix race in which he had crashed and broken his back. Pressure on another button propelled the electric chair towards her and he stopped a few feet away.

'So you got the sponsorship?' was his only greeting.

'Yes, I got it.'

'Good. Then we're one stage further on. Now all you have to do is win it.' His voice was harsh, abrasive— but it had always been like that, ever since she could remember, it was only to Bill or others of his old friends that he permitted to visit him that his voice was ever warm, polite even. Dimly she could recall him once having been loving and affectionate, but only towards her mother, never to Toni. Because it was Toni he blamed for the two great tragedies in his life.

She looked at him now and said abruptly, 'There are conditions.'

His eyes narrowed. 'Well?'

'One concerns Bill.'

'All right. We'll go outside.'

He propelled himself into the open, too proud ever to let anyone push the chair, fiercely clinging on to the little independence the buttons gave him. He stopped near the old rockery, a blaze of red and orange rock-roses, with here and there, the blue of lavender and forget-me-nots fighting to reach the sun among the dense growth.

'Well?' he asked again.

Briefly Toni outlined the idea for the film.

He nodded in approval. 'It's far better than I hoped. But you had no right to ask for more than I told you to,' he added irritably. 'You could have lost everything.'

Toni looked at him sitting in the wheelchair, his face lined with the years of pain, his hair prematurely grey, making him look old when he was still under fifty. Only his eyes were alive; they shone with the burning, compulsive ambition that filled his wasted body. Before his accident his one all-consuming aim in life had been to win the Grand Prix Racing Championship and his life had been completely devoted to that end, then, just as the championship seemed within his grasp, his wife had died trying to give him the son he so badly wanted to carry on his name. She died only the day before the race that would decide the championship, but he had taken part in it anyway, but his concentration was impaired and he had crashed. Although she had only been eight then Toni could still remember the way he had looked when they told him her mother was dead. Then he had turned on Toni, his face savage, and said, 'If you'd been born a boy she wouldn't have kept trying to have another child. She wouldn't have died!' And when he at last came home from hospital after the crash he had made it plain to her, without actually putting it into words, that he also blamed her for his accident, shutting her out of his life completely. But then Bill, his old mechanic, came to live with them and the ambition took a new form. Together they would develop a new Formula One racing car—and Toni was to drive it! She had leapt at the idea, pathetically eager to find some way to please her father, trying desperately to prove herself as good as the son he had wanted so badly, hoping always for some sign of affection, a word of praise.

So she had learned to drive before she was fifteen, roaring round the track in the field behind the house, passed her driving test on her seventeenth birthday and took part in a competition rally only a week later. But not in her own name—he wouldn't allow that; he was too proud of the Drake family name to let her use it in case she failed, so instead she used her mother's maiden name of Wyndham. Meanwhile every penny that her father could find went into the building of a prototype racing car, with the result that the house and everything else was neglected. As soon as she left school, Toni looked round for the kind of job that would fit round her driving, and was lucky enough to be taken on by a model agency.

'What about Bill?' he demanded.

'They don't want him, they want to use their own

chief mechanic. They wouldn't entertain the idea otherwise.'

Her father considered briefly, then dismissed Bill out of hand. 'All right, I'll tell him. What else?'

'They want their own navigator, too.' Somehow Toni felt unable at this stage to tell him just who the navigator was to be.

'Is he any good?'

'They say he's experienced.'

'Humph! That could mean anything. You'll just have to go over the course yourself and double check on anything he does.'

They started to talk about the rally in more detail and then went to look at the latest work they had done on the racing car. With only Bill able to do the practical work progress was slow, and the prototype had been altered several times over the years as new design rules and ideas came into being. Toni looked at the car with the usual welter of emotions she always felt whenever she saw it. A gripping anticipation that tied her stomach in knots and made her hands shake as she sat in the driving seat that had been especially modified to fit her, the pedals at a comfortable distance for her feet, the gear lever close by her left hand. Her hands gripped the steering-wheel tightly and for a moment she let herself imagine what it would be like to take part in a Formula One race; almost she could hear the screaming whine of the engine as it tore along the track at well over a hundred miles an hour, drowning out the roar of the crowds of spectators; could see the hairpin bends and chicanes opening up before her as she tried to take the car faster, always faster, through the twists and turns of the racing circuit.

'Toni?'

Her name was said on a sharp, questioning note and she looked up to find her father watching her frowningly. Deliberately she forced herself to relax and ask the question he wanted to hear. 'When will it be ready? How much longer do I have to wait?'

The frown was replaced by a look of satisfaction and he started to give her details of their progress, but Toni hardly listened; she gave a small, inner sigh of relief because he still didn't suspect that she was at all unsure of herself, that she was afraid to even dare to try and analyse her own emotions in case she found out that what she felt was not nervous excitement and anticipation — but stark fear!

Shortly afterwards she made the excuse that she had an early modelling assignment the next day and left, driving back to London as fast as the speed limit allowed, eager to get away from her father's fanaticism and back to her own life. When she let herself into the apartment, Carinna was in her usual position — curled up on the settee in her housecoat, talking on the telephone, and by the comfortable way she was lounging, had been doing so for some time.

She raised a languid hand to Toni and said into the receiver, 'Why, *Adam*, that sounds absolutely fascinating,' emphasising the name to let Toni know who she was speaking to.

Toni raised her eyebrows and hissed, 'Does he want me?'

Carinna shook her head, at the same time giving an amused laugh into the phone as if in answer to a joke or witticism.

Toni left her to it and went into her room to change into casual jeans and a sweater.

When she came back into the room Carinna was just

putting down the receiver. 'That was Adam York,' she said unnecessarily.

'You seem to have forgotten the prefix,' Toni reminded her drily.

Carinna frowned. 'What prefix?'

'You used to call him "*your* Adam York".'

'Oh! Yes, well ... It was perfectly obvious that you weren't interested in him, so I ... er ...'

'So you decided to make a play for him,' Toni filled in for her.

'And why not?' Carinna was immediately on the defensive. 'Just because you dislike him it doesn't mean that I have to as well. In case you hadn't noticed he's *very* good-looking, quite macho in fact—*and* he's rich. Do you know that he owns a controlling interest in Century Vision?'

'No, I didn't know. And although that fact might make him more attractive in your eyes, it doesn't in mine. He just uses the power that his wealth gives him to blackmail people into letting him get his own way.' Toni paused, then asked, 'What did he want, anyway?'

'Oh, he wasn't phoning us—I called him to thank him for inviting me to the Wayne Robertson party,' Carinna answered offhandedly.

'You're chasing him,' Toni said accusingly.

Carinna immediately fired back, 'No, I'm not. It was merely a thank you call.'

'Oh, yes, you are. I can always tell when you decide to chase a man—you start gushing all over him.'

Her face flushed, Carinna got angrily to her feet. 'I do not gush! I'm just looking out for my future, that's all. My legs aren't going to be photographable for ever, and nor are yours!'

'So then I'll find some other way of earning a living,'

Toni retorted. 'I'm my own mistress, and I certainly don't intend to stoop to running after men!'

Carinna snorted triumphantly. 'You're becoming such an arrant feminist that soon no man will even *want* you as *his* mistress! *And* there's no need to take it out on me just because you had to visit your father today.'

Toni stared at her, her face suddenly stricken. 'Was *that* what I was doing? Oh, hell! Carinna, I'm sorry, I didn't mean it.'

Her roommate sat down again. 'It doesn't matter. Maybe you're right, maybe I do make it too obvious that I'm interested in a man. I certainly never seem to land one.' Moodily she got up and went over to the cupboard to pour out a couple of drinks.

'Nonsense,' Toni retorted encouragingly. 'What about that industrialist you went out with for a few months every time he came to London? He proposed to you— *and* he was rolling in money?'

'I know,' Carinna handed her a glass. 'But it was his father who controlled all the purse-strings—and besides, when he kissed me it was like being kissed by a sink plunger!' And then she burst into delighted laughter at the stunned look on Toni's face.

After that, they were back in their usual friendly intimacy again and talked of other things, but just before they went to bed, Carinna said rather uncomfortably, 'I suppose I'd better confess. I tried to coax Adam York into letting me go with you on Tuesday when you pick up the car.'

'Carinna! That's purely business.'

'I know, but Adam will be there, and I want to see him again. I really like him, Toni,' she added earnestly.

'What did he say?' Toni demanded.

'Well—he said it was okay by him as long as you didn't mind,' Carinna admitted.

Toni looked at her friend somewhat exasperatedly. 'All right, you can come along. Maybe it won't be such a bad idea, after all—you can keep him out of my hair while I'm busy with the car. I certainly don't want him interfering in something he knows nothing about.' Then, crossing to put her hand on Carinna's arm, she said, 'And if you really think that something could come of it, then I'll do everything I can to help.'

Carinna gave her an impulsive hug of gratitude, but later, as Toni undressed for bed, the old adage 'Fools rush in where angels fear to tread' came strongly into her mind and she doubted very much whether she was doing her friend a favour in helping her to hook Adam York!

CHAPTER THREE

On Tuesday, when Toni and Carinna, escorted by Steve Landors, were shown into the Sales Manager's office at the car factory, they found that Adam York was there before them, a drink in his hand, and a masculine air of conviviality amongst the men in the room. An atmosphere which was almost physically put aside as every eye turned on the girls and the men began to automatically stand up to greet them, to straighten their ties and to generally preen themselves like parading peacocks. Only Adam seemed immune to the impression they created. He got languidly to his feet and performed the necessary introductions, leaving Toni open to the usual clichés from one or two of the men: 'You're much too fragile to be a rally driver', and 'Not a very feminine hobby for a pretty thing like you, m'dear'. All said in a tone that was meant to convey gallantry, but which only served to put Toni's teeth on edge. The head of the Motor Racing Division, however, was of a different calibre; he made no attempt to be smooth but told her of some of the famous women drivers he had met and also about their own women's driving team that the company were in the process of training.

'Do you intend to take up rallying as a career?' he asked her.

Toni shook her head. 'No, I'd rather go on to motor racing. I've been offered the chance to drive a works Formula Three car if I do well in the Royal Car Club Rally.'

As she spoke, she felt someone come up behind her and turned to find Adam almost at her elbow. He handed her a drink with a brief nod and then walked away, and Toni wondered rather uneasily if he had heard. Not that it mattered, it wasn't any secret, but it did occur to her belatedly to wonder if he might resent having his company's sponsorship used as a means to an end.

After the drinks they all went down to one of the bays where the film crew was waiting and where the director of the documentary told them what he wanted them to do. Steve and Toni had to go outside and pretend to drive up to the factory again and there be met by the Racing and Sales Managers who led them into the factory where they walked down the assembly line and were eventually presented with an Escort at the rolling-chassis stage, without an engine or gear-box. There was a pause for the crew to resight their cameras and then Toni and Steve got down to the important part of discussing what amendments they wanted to turn the Escort into a vehicle tough enough to withstand extremely rough terrain, but also fast enough to win them the rally.

At first Toni felt extremely conscious of the cameras hovering in the background the whole time, often looking over her shoulder, and it took a great effort not to look directly at them and to keep her voice at the right pitch, not too high so that it sounded unnatural, and not too low so that the microphones couldn't pick it up. And the fact that Adam, Carinna, and several of the firm's directors were standing there watching, didn't help any. She had been surprised to find that Adam wasn't taking part, but the director had explained that they would do a piece on him demonstrating all the navigational aids and gadgets later on after they had been fitted into the car. Gradually her intense interest in what she was discussing made her almost forget the cameras, only really noticing them when they got in the way.

The Racing Manager was taking down a list of all the amendments she wanted, and remarked, 'We have a standard bumpguard which we can fit for the more rugged parts of the course, but it can be removed for the racing stages.'

'Good,' Toni said approvingly. 'And I'll also want the suspension stiffened so that it will hold the road better.'

'What about the safety factor?'

'We'll want a laminated windshield, of course. A dual braking system and the fuel tank covered in fire proof material.'

'And of course you'll want the full roll-cage,' Steve reminded her.

Toni shook her head. 'Too heavy. Just a roll-bar over the front seats will be sufficient.'

They went on to discuss the technical details of the engine and gearbox for another half an hour or more, and then fixed a date for Toni and Steve to come and inspect the modifications. The camera crew packed up and left for another assignment, but Toni, Carinna, Adam and Steve were invited to have lunch with the directors. Toni found herself placed between the Racing Manager and Adam, while Carinna made sure that she was at his other side with Steve as her left-hand neighbour.

'I hope you didn't find being filmed too intimidating,' Adam remarked.

'I did at first,' Toni admitted. 'But, like everything

else, you get used to it after a while.'

A slight look of amusement came into his grey eyes. 'Oh, I'm sure that there are some things you never get used to—or life would become very dull.'

Toni flushed slightly, wondering whether he was making fun of her. 'I don't know what you mean,' she answered stiffly.

His left eyebrow rose quizzically, 'Don't you?' Then, almost to himself as his eyes studied her, 'No, perhaps you don't.'

But then Carinna claimed his attention and Toni was relieved to be free of him. Somehow he had the ability to make her feel like a gauche schoolgirl. She concentrated on talking solely to the Racing Manager, her shoulder resolutely turned away from Adam, but when the dessert was served, she was obliged to pass him the cream jug.

'You seem to find the subject of cars totally absorbing,' he remarked with a somewhat wry twist to his mouth. 'Don't you have any other interests?'

'Oh, no,' Toni returned blithely. 'I have a one-track mind, but—unlike men—mine happens to be a racing track. But Carinna has lots of interests. Why don't you ask her? I'm sure she'd love to tell you.'

His face hardened. 'You think you're a very tough young lady, don't you?'

Toni's chin came up. 'Yes,' she answered. 'I do—and I *am*.'

Grey eyes met violet in a distinct challenge. Silkily he said, 'Well, that's something you're going to have to prove one way or another.'

Ten days later Toni swept through the double doors leading to Adam York's office, past his startled receptionist, and threw open the door of his inner sanctum without bothering to knock. He was seated behind his vast desk, with a secretary opposite taking down dictation. They both looked up as she stormed in, the secretary's mouth gaping open in amazement.

'I want a word with you,' Toni informed him furiously.

Adam's jaw tightened, but after a moment he turned to the secretary and said, 'All right, Jane; we'll finish the letters later.'

Toni tapped her foot impatiently until she heard the door click shut behind the girl, then she strode angrily across and planted her hands on his desk, glowering down at him. 'Now you listen to me, Adam York! If you ...'

He came to his feet, displeasure in his face, and spoke at the same time. 'Just what right do you think you've got to come slamming into my office?'

'What right? I'll *tell* you what right,' Toni returned furiously. 'You went down to the factory behind my back and altered my modifications to the car. You may be able to interfere and throw your weight around in the television studios, but *I'm* driving that car and I insist on having it made to *my* specification.'

'To what, exactly, are you referring?' he asked coldly.

'You know damn well what I mean,' she fumed. 'You told them to put in a full roll-cage when I specifically asked for just a roll-*bar*. *And* you told them to put a seat in the back. What do you think we're entering for the rally—a taxi?' She added scornfully, 'You may not know the first thing about rallying, but I should have thought even a schoolboy would know that you need the rear of the car to stow your gear in!'

He came round the desk towards her, his stride purposeful, but Toni stood her ground.

'Let's get something straight, once and for all,' she snapped. 'The fact that you're sponsoring me doesn't give you the right to interfere in any way with the arrangements I make for the car, the service crew, or anything else connected with the rally. Is that quite clear?'

Adam's mouth drew into a thin line. 'Oh, you make yourself perfectly plain. But I have no intention of allowing you to make decisions which affect the safety factors of the car.'

'If by that you mean the roll-cage, then you've obviously been listening to people who don't know what they're talking about. A roll-bar is perfectly adequate for protection should the car turn over.'

He might not have heard her. 'The roll-cage stays.'

Toni snorted with exasperation and then said with exaggerated patience, as if she was explaining to a rather backward child, 'Look, the whole point of the rally is that you have to drive the car at fast speeds. Therefore the lighter the car the better. But you have to carry a lot of gear: spare tires, tools, equipment, that sort of thing. So you throw out as much unnecessary weight as you can. And a full roll-cage is just not necessary. Believe me, I've taken part in dozens of rallies and I know.'

Adam shook his head. 'I'm sorry. It stays.'

Toni glared at him, her eyes blazing with anger. 'Just who is driving this car?'

Quite unperturbed, he replied steadily, 'You are. And I'm going to make sure that you drive it to the finish without breaking your silly young neck.'

'My neck?' She gave a scornful laugh. 'Why don't

you admit that it's your own neck you're *afraid* for?'

His jaw tightened and for the first time anger showed in his face. For a moment he looked as if he was about to make some withering retort, but held himself in control and merely said, 'I'll overlook your rudeness this time because you have a right to be angry; I shouldn't have made the alterations without referring to you first, but...'

'You shouldn't have made them at all!' Toni flashed.

'But when I tried to contact you at your apartment I couldn't get any reply, so—rather than do the job twice—I told the factory to put in the full roll-cage. If you hadn't gone down to the factory before we arranged you would have received the letter I sent to you yesterday explaining my action.'

Toni drew herself up and glared at him. 'I don't give a damn for your reasons! I want the roll-cage out.'

Adam returned her look, his face set and hard. 'It stays—or I withdraw my company's sponsorship.'

She gave a little gasp as if he'd hit her. 'You wouldn't dare!'

'Try me,' he answered coldly.

'But—but that's downright blackmail!'

'Is it? Personally I prefer to call it common sense.'

Toni stared at him for a moment, her face tense and pale, then she swung away from him and walked quickly across to the window and gazed out of it, her back towards him.

For several minutes neither of them spoke; Toni looking blindly out over the rooftops, Adam standing watching her, then he broke the silence by saying in a matter-of-fact tone, 'The rear seat has been left in only temporarily. It's to allow a cameraman to film you taking the car over some practice runs. During the rally it will be taken out and an automatic camera and microphone rigged up in its place.' He paused, but when she didn't move added, 'I trust you have no objection to that?'

At last she turned to face him, her eyes over-bright, her hands balled into fists at her side, but her emotions held in rigid check. 'Sure, go ahead,' she said with cold flippancy. 'But why bother to take out the seat? Why not just cram the whole camera crew in the back? With an overweight car and an amateur navigator who's chicken into the bargain, we don't stand a hope in hell of winning anyway!'

And before he could make a move to stop her, she had turned on her heel and marched out of the room.

The next filming session at the factory was an entirely different occasion from the first; the car company's big brass didn't put in an appearance and nor did Adam, which meant, of course, that Carinna didn't bother to come either. Which left only Steve and Toni and a couple of experts from the Racing Division to examine the car and be interviewed. Which was just as well, because Toni still felt so angry over the car that she would have been quite unable to pretend that nothing had happened if Adam had been there—gloating over his triumph, she thought viciously.

Afterwards she drove Steve back to town, in her car this time, and they stopped off at a pub for a basket meal.

'What would you like to drink?' he asked her.

'Oh, beer, please.'

He brought the two pints of frothy-headed beer back to their table and grinned at her. 'You're a strange girl, you know that?'

'Because I drink beer?' Toni wiped away the white moustache that the froth had left.

'Partly that.'

'But lots of women drink beer.'

'Not girls who look like you and Carinna. Too many calories.'

Toni smiled at him. 'You'd be surprised. It's cheap and it's thirst-quenching. Both Carinna and I like it, although I don't attempt to drink more than one or two during the course of an evening.'

'At that chat-show party Carinna only drank shorts.'

'Mm, but she usually chooses her drinks to match her company.'

'I see.'

Toni looked at Steve thoughtfully; she had noticed him watching Carinna more than once, and when they talked he often brought the conversation round to her. It was perfectly natural, of course, Carinna was extremely attractive, but Toni knew her friend well enough to know that with Adam York around, Steve didn't stand a chance, even though he was handsome in a casual kind of way and had a much more pleasant personality. But beside Adam's suave charm and his immense bank balance, Steve didn't even come into the picture.

She sighed and said, 'You like Carinna, don't you?'

He gave a wry grin. 'And some! She's the loveliest thing I've ever seen.' He recollected himself hastily and added, 'Don't get me wrong, you're beautiful too, but —well, I suppose some gentlemen prefer blondes.'

Oh, dear, he really had got it badly, Toni thought, as she tried to find some way of letting him down gently. Slowly she said, 'And isn't it possible that some blondes prefer—gentlemen, in the old-fashioned sense of the word?'

Steve was silent for a moment as he took in the implication, then said gruffly, 'You mean rich men, right?'

'I'm afraid so.'

Lifting his glass, he drained it and then said, 'Thanks for the tip, saves me making a fool of myself. I was afraid of something like that. She's much too classy a lady ever to be satisfied with a glorified mechanic. Is there anyone in particular she's after?'

'There may be, it's too early to say,' Toni answered cautiously.

He set down his glass. 'How about you? Are you playing the same game?'

Toni held up her hands in horror. 'Heaven forbid! I'm definitely in the anti-marriage league.'

A sudden grin split Steve's face. 'Then I think I'll join the club!'

The next two or three weeks were extremely busy ones for Toni; even though much of the pleasure and excitement had gone out of the preparations for the rally, she still did what was expected of her to the best of her ability. She now had little hope of winning, but the television coverage would be useful in promoting her career and getting her name known, so she worked to that end—firmly shutting out of her mind the possibility that if her showing in the rally was a dismal failure, that, too, would be widely known.

She gave several interviews to the motoring press and appeared on an afternoon women's programme on radio, as well as making frequent checks on the progress of the car, conferring with Steve to decide the best positions on the route to place the service vans and

arranging for trials for the car as soon as it was handed
over to her. On top of all this, of course, she also had to
cram in as many modelling assignments as she could
in order to get some savings together to pay her rent
for the weeks when she couldn't work because she
would be busy with practice runs. Her expenses during
the rally itself, though, would be paid by Century
Vision, so that was one load off her mind.

During this time she saw nothing of Adam York, his
secretary having advised her that he had gone to
America on business. Which suited Toni very well; at
least he couldn't interfere from that distance, and she
fervently hoped that she would have to see as little as
possible of him until the rally in November. Carinna,
of course, took the opposite view, but it didn't stop her
from dating someone else while he was away, Toni
noted cynically.

Because of her motoring connections, Toni was
offered an assignment at Brands Hatch, modelling
some rather way-out clothes by an Italian designer who
was trying to establish a fashion house in London.
Brands Hatch was chosen because there was a Formula
One meeting there in which several Italian works teams
were taking part and the designer wanted the models
photographed against a background of the Italian racing cars with some of the drivers also appearing in the
pictures.

It was a two to three-day assignment, largely de-
pendent on the weather, with some of the shots to be
taken very early in the morning before the track was
opened to the public, so everyone was booked into a
local hotel. On the first day the cars were only practis-
ing and building up their lap times to get the best places
at the starting grid, so some of the drivers had time to

spare for the photographers, and they progressed quite
well until the sky started to cloud over and they kept
having to stop and wait for the sun to come out again.

During one of these waits Toni was standing by a
young Italian named Gino Moroni, who was in his first
season as a Formula One driver and, as he spoke good
English, she was soon asking him about his car, which
formed the background of the shot. Without letting
him know that she had done any professional driving
herself, she started to admire the racing car and he
rather condescendingly offered to let her sit in it, as if
he was doing her a great favour. Toni played up to this
by pretending to be terribly impressed and asking naïve
questions about the dashboard instruments and engine,
and flattering him extravagantly about how brave
and clever he must be to take part in such a dangerous
sport. He lapped it up, enjoying every fulsome word
she said—and believing it too!

He began to flirt with her and Toni quite deliberately encouraged him, using her sex to get him interested and wanting more. Using him as men so often
had tried to use her. Being an Italian, Gino was only
a little taller than Toni in her high heels, but he was
handsome in a Latin kind of way, with thick, dark
wavy hair, and dazzlingly white teeth in his smiling,
olive-skinned face, tanned even darker by the sun. He
was still so new to the upper echelons of the motor-
racing fraternity that he hadn't yet become blasé and
bored with the crowds of girls who hung about the
Grand Prix circuits, willing to do anything to get to
know their heroes—the Formula One men, the super-
men of racing. So Toni found no great difficulty in
hooking him on her line, gazing at him admiringly
from eyes that were deep, mysterious violet pools, eyes

that were both innocent and yet full of promise. By the end of the day she had him just where she wanted him —eating out of her hand!

When the light finally went and the photo session broke up, Gino drew her to one side, out of sight. Putting an arm round her waist, he drew her to him and began to kiss her neck. Toni pretended to giggle girlishly and half-heartedly told him to stop.

'If only I did not have the race tomorrow,' Gino groaned. 'Then we could spend the night together and I would show you how an Italian makes love—and never again would you want to go to bed with any of your cold-blooded Englishmen,' he boasted.

And he really believes that! Toni thought in amazement, then caught his hand as it started to wander too far and carried it up to her cheek, looking at him soulfully. 'You mean we can't?' she asked, her voice heavy with disappointment.

He shook his head. 'No, *cara*. We are not allowed any—fun the day before a race. And I have to be up at dawn to give the car a last test round the circuit before the race. But tomorrow night ...' His hand slid down to her hips and pressed her hard against him, while he leered down at her lasciviously.

But Toni quickly stepped back and said excitedly, as if she'd just had a sudden idea, 'You have to be here early in the morning? But so do we. We're taking a lot of shots before the place gets too busy. I'll be able to wish you luck before the race.'

She let him kiss her again then, as a sample of the goodies he obviously expected to fall into his bed the following night, and he went strutting away, whistling, while Toni looked after him, a satisfied little smile on her face.

But later that evening, after they had been driven back to the hotel and had changed for dinner, Toni and the girl she was sharing a room with walked into the bar to meet the rest of the crew and the first person Toni saw was Adam York, in close conversation with the photographer! He looked up as she came in and after she had got over the first shock of surprise, Toni went to give him only a small nod of recognition and walk over to the others who were standing some way apart, but Adam said a brief word to the photographer and moved forward to meet her.

'Hallo, Toni. Let me get you a drink.'

'Thanks, but as you can see, I'm with a crowd.' She tried to move away, but he put a hand under her elbow and led her towards an empty table.

'It's all right, I've already explained to your boss that I want to talk to you.'

'Have you really?' Toni said tartly. 'And I suppose it never occurred to you that I might not want to talk to you?' She tried to pull away. 'Will you please let go of my arm? I'm quite capable of walking without you holding on to me like some kind of jailer.'

He let go of her at once and shrugged. 'Sorry. It's just habit for a man to help a woman along.'

'*Some* women are capable of managing perfectly well by themselves,' Toni replied forcefully, and deliberately pulled a chair out for herself, before he could do it for her.

Adam settled himself in the opposite seat and looked at her sardonically. 'Am I allowed to buy you a drink, or are you going to insist on buying that for yourself too?'

A flash of anger came into Toni's eyes. 'You can buy the first round. I'll buy the second.' Not that I intend to talk to you a minute longer than I have to, she added to herself.

He gave their order to the waiter, then turned towards her again. 'I expect you're wondering why I'm here?'

Toni shrugged. 'I hadn't thought about it—to cover the big race, I suppose.'

He shook his head. 'No. I called Carinna and she told me that you were here and what you were doing, and it gave me an idea for a sequence in our film.'

So he had rung Carinna, presumably to make a date, Toni conjectured, so that relationship looked as if it was heading in the right direction. Although how Carinna could even contemplate marriage with such a cold, autocratic despot, Toni couldn't imagine; he would probably have his secretary make an appointment every time he decided to sleep with his wife, she decided cynically.

The ridiculousness of the thought made her eyes light up with hastily-suppressed laughter, and Adam's brows rose. 'Care to share the joke?'

She shook her head. 'I don't think you'd appreciate it, somehow.'

His lips compressed into a thin line. 'Which probably means it was at my expense.'

Toni sat back in her chair and looked at him tauntingly. 'Wouldn't you like to know?'

His eyes returned her look coldly. 'Not particularly. I hardly think that your brand of humour is likely to appeal to me. Now, do you intend to spend the whole evening trying to provoke me, or shall we get down to business?'

Making no attempt to hide her dislike for him, Toni

replied, 'Oh, by all means let's get this over and done with as quickly as possible.'

'Very well. I've arranged for the film crew to come here tomorrow. They'll film you being photographed against the background of the race track and then do a short interview about the modelling aspect of your life. I trust you have no objection to that?' he added drily.

'I take it that you've already okayed this with the fashion photographer?'

Adam nodded. 'He welcomes the extra publicity.'

'Then who am I to object?' Toni said derisively. 'It's written into my contract with you that I have to make myself available for filming whenever necessary. What it doesn't say, of course, is that I have to like being manipulated.'

She stood up to go, but Adam said brusquely, 'Sit down. I haven't finished yet.'

For a moment Toni glared at him defiantly, but then slowly obeyed him as the waiter came up with their drinks.

Adam signed the bill and went on, 'The factory will have the Escort ready for collection on Saturday. Have you decided where and when you want to do the trials?'

Toni's reply was prompt and businesslike. 'Yes, there's a test-track on the Welsh border that covers both forest and hill country. I want to have a week there with the service crew so that we'll know exactly what we've got to face, and the crew can practise fast engine changes, repairs, that kind of thing. Then I'd need at least another week at a closed race-track or disused airfield getting the steering and weight right for the road stages. So I shall need to know your weight,' she added, her eyes running critically over his long but compact body.

'It's one hundred seventy pounds, near enough.'

'In that case our combined weight will be unevenly distributed and I'll have to compensate for it by having all the heavy stuff on my side of the car to start with, but we'll be able to move some over as the rally progresses.'

'Oh, really? Why?'

Toni regarded him mockingly. 'Because you'll lose at least seven pounds during the course of the rally. Unfortunately there isn't time to stop for three-hour business lunches every day.'

'I hadn't supposed there would be,' he returned drily. 'But if I lose weight, then so will you.'

She shook her head. 'I'm a professional; I keep myself fit. Whereas you—you'll just be a *passenger*,' she emphasised insultingly.

Adam's brows drew together into an angry frown, but he merely said shortly, 'Give me the address and date on which you want the car delivered and I'll see that the arrangements are made.'

Toni stood up again. 'That won't be necessary. *I've* already told the factory exactly what *I* want done with the car. Goodnight, Mr York.' And with a feeling of intense satisfaction, she turned on her heel and without a backward glance walked across the room to join her colleagues.

The first raw bite of winter hung in the air when Toni arrived at the race-track very early the following morning, accompanied only by a young apprentice photographer, Pete, whom she had wheedled into doing what she wanted. At first he had demurred, but then the sheer madness of what she intended had aroused his curiosity and he had agreed to come along.

'Now you're sure you know what to do?' Toni asked

for the third time as they walked along to the pits. 'Just keep him busy for those few minutes.'

'Sure, I know what to do. Look, there he is now.'

He pointed to where Gino Moroni was standing by his car, dressed in his racing overalls, and talking to a mechanic. As soon as Gino saw Toni he came over and kissed her, his arm going possessively round her waist.

'You got up so early to come and watch me, *cara*?'

'Oh, I didn't want to miss even a minute,' Toni assured him, gazing up at him adoringly. 'Is your car all ready to go?' When he nodded, she clung to his arm and said, 'Oh, Gino, you know yesterday you let me sit in the car? Well, I thought how fantastic it would be if I could have my photo taken in it, so I brought Pete along to take a few shots.' She indicated the photographer with a wave of her hand and said huskily, 'You don't mind, do you, Gino darling?'

Gino stroked her arm fondly. 'Of course not, *cara*, but you must hurry before the rest of the team arrive.'

Pete, carefully primed, said, 'Hey, Toni, why don't you put on the overalls and helmet; that would make a really good picture?'

Toni clapped her hands excitedly. 'Of course. What a wonderful idea!'

In no time at all, Gino had been persuaded to find her a pair of overalls which Toni slipped on over the sweater and jeans she was wearing, and then he passed over his own helmet and helped her to fit it on.

Climbing into the car, Toni smiled up at him. 'Do I look the part?'

'You look wonderful, *cara*. But hurry, please, and don't touch anything,' he added rather nervously as he glanced at his watch.

'Just show me how to do up the straps,' Toni coaxed.

'Oh, and you must lend me your gloves,'

He did so, and while Toni was pulling on the special Nomex flame-resistant gloves, she nodded across to Pete. 'Okay, I'm ready.'

Pete pretended to take a shot, then fiddled with the camera. 'Oh, hell, the film's got stuck.' He wrestled with it, then said, 'Do you know anything about cameras, Gino?'

Gino probably didn't, but being young, male, and Italian, he wasn't going to admit that and went across to sort it out.

'Perhaps we'd better move out of the light?' Pete suggested. 'We don't want to ruin the film.' He led the way into the dim recesses of the pits, Gino following like a lamb.

Toni pulled down the visor of the helmet and took a deep breath. The track opened like a long ribbon before her, the mist curling along it as the morning sun warmed the dew-soaked earth. Putting her hands on the wheel, she let her nostrils fill with the familiar smell of petrol and oil, the lingering odour of exhaust fumes that were never quite dispelled. Reaching out to the instrument panel she found that she was a little short for the cockpit which had been designed to fit round Gino, but that couldn't be helped, she would have to manage. She gave a quick glance to see that Pete was still keeping him occupied and turned on the engine, at the same time revving the accelerator and pushing the stick into first gear. It started with a great, throaty roar that shattered the dawn silence and covered Gino's startled shout. He started to run towards her, but Pete deliberately got in his way. Angrily he pushed Pete aside and ran out of the pits while Toni fumbled a little at the unfamiliar controls, but almost as he reached her, Toni swung out of the pits and on to the empty track, her foot down hard on the accelerator.

It wasn't the first time Toni had driven round Brands Hatch; she had taken part in several ladies' races and a couple of Formula Ford races there, but always on the shorter Club circuit, never on the full Grand Prix circuit of 2.6 miles, and never before in a car capable of such high speeds. Taking Gino's car had been a mad thing to do, she knew, but she *had* to know, *had* to find out for herself, just what those feelings were that she experienced every time she sat in her father's prototype racing car.

Something of those feelings came to her now as the speedometer crept up to eighty, ninety. Still unfamiliar with the car, she daren't go any faster down Hailwood Hill and changed down to take the hairpin at Druid's Bend, but gained more confidence as she roared into the long, long straight of Pilgrim's Drop, the needle pushing well up over a hundred now. Even with the crash helmet on the noise of the engine was deafening and she could feel the powerful engine vibrating through the steering-wheel. Dropping into Hawthorn Hill and round the bend, she entered another straight and pressed her foot down even harder, taking the next gradual bend at little under a hundred. Then along Dingle Dell, into the sharp right at the corner and then left into Stirling's Bend and into the long straight to Clark Curve which led towards the pits again. Toni's mouth tightened grimly; she was going fast but not fast enough. This car had only a normal racing engine, whereas her father's prototype was turbo-charged and would probably go even faster, and she just *had* to find out whether she was capable of handling that kind of speed, and find out now in the comparative privacy of the empty track, not in the prototype car when her father would be watching her.

Well, there was only one way for her to find out what her personal limits were, and that was to drive beyond them. Toni went into Brabham Straight faster than she had ever driven anything in her life. As she passed the pits she caught a glimpse of several people waving at her frantically, but they hardly registered; she was putting all her concentration into the blind flat-out approach to Paddock Bend with the fast downhill exit behind it. The car seemed to drop down the hill faster than light, the ground rushing away beneath her, the engine roaring in her ears. Then the hairpin. Toni changed down, but not quickly enough. The car seemed to become a live thing, a monster that tried to take control and tear the steering-wheel from her hands. Grimly she fought it, desperately braking and trying to turn the wheel, the tires screaming. And the fear was there inside her, a tangible thing, that made her want to cry out and let go, to give up the unequal struggle against this machine that wanted to destroy her. The car roared up on to the nearside wheels and for a terrifying instant she thought that she'd lost it, but then, by some miracle, it righted itself and she was out of the hairpin and heading for the straight again.

She took the rest of the lap very fast, in complete control of the car, but when she drew up at the pits the terror was still there, raw in her mind, in her shaking hands and trembling body.

Gino was among the first to reach her; he was almost jumping up and down with rage, screaming abuse at her in Italian, but Toni was almost unaware of him. She switched off the engine, took off the helmet, and went to pull herself out of the car, but then fell back,

all the strength suddenly gone from her limbs. A man
pushed Gino forcibly aside and reached into the car
to lift her out bodily. He carried her through the
crowd of men, into the pits and on into an office at the
back where he firmly kicked the door shut in the face
of the people trying to follow, and then set her down on
her feet. Only then did Toni realise it was Adam.

The moment he let go of her her legs gave way and
she started to fall, so he caught hold of her arm to hold
her up.

'You crazy little fool! You could have killed yourself
out there! What in hell possessed you to do such a
brainless thing?' He was shouting at her, his face dark
with fury, his usual coldness lost beneath the raging
heat of his anger.

When she didn't answer at once he caught hold of
her arms and shook her. 'Answer me! Why the hell did
you pull such a crazy trick?'

Toni blinked at him, still feeling dazed and weak.
She tried ineffectively to free herself, at the same time
cringing away from his anger. 'It was—it was something I had to do,' she managed, her voice husky and
unsteady. 'I had to—to find out. Had to know.'

'What did you have to find out? What was it? Tell
me!' The fingers bit into her flesh and he pulled her
closer to him, his eyes searching her face intently.

'What?' Slowly Toni began to realise where she was,
who she was with. 'What are *you* doing here?'

'That doesn't matter,' he answered dismissively,
then, urgently, 'Toni, you have to tell me—why did
you take the car? What was it you were trying to find
out?'

But her senses were coming back to her fast now and
she was on her guard. What she had discovered about

herself, out there on the track, was not to be shared with anyone, ever. A shutter came down over her face as she said coldly, 'Please let go of me, you're hurting my arms.'

But he didn't let go, if anything his grip tightened. 'Not until you tell me why you had to take that car.'

Toni managed a brittle laugh. 'Just for the hell of it, of course. A joy-ride, if ...'

'Don't lie to me!' Adam's eyes blazed with anger. 'You took that car because you wanted to prove something about yourself. Didn't you?' he demanded savagely.

'Oh, really!' Toni drew herself up and glared at him. 'All this fuss because I tricked Gino into letting me try his car out. I do have an International Licence, you know. I was only trying the thing out for size!'

Adam's eyes raked her face. 'Were you? Or were you trying yourself out for size, finding out whether *you* were big enough for the car?'

'Oh, for heaven's sake! What are you—some kind of amateur psychiatrist? I took the car because I'd never driven a Formula One machine before, and that's all! Don't read something into it that isn't there.' She changed from defence to attack. 'And just why are *you* so all-fired angry about it, anyway? Anyone would think that you were worried about me,' she added sardonically.

Abruptly Adam let go of her and stepped back. His tone equally scathing, he said shortly, 'My company has a great deal of money invested in you which I don't intend to see wasted. If you're stupid enough to risk your neck, then do so by all means—but *not* until after the R.C.C. rally!'

Toni looked at him with a wry twist to her mouth

and said nastily, 'Oh, that's better. That's far more like your usual pompous self!'

His mouth thinned and a closed look came over his face. 'I want your promise that you won't pull this kind of stunt again or take any other unnecessary risks. Is that understood?'

'Yes, all right!' Toni shouted back at him impatiently, but she gave the promise easily enough; she knew everything there was to know—now.

'Good.' Adam moved towards the door, then turned to look back at her. 'Tell me, what cheap trick did you pull to get the Italian to let you drive his car? I bet you promised him everything he wanted—but never intended to let him even touch you?' he added sneeringly.

Toni was so taken aback by the truth of his accusation that for a moment she couldn't speak, and, before she could answer, his eyes swept over her contemptuously and he strode out of the room.

An abject apology and blatant femininity not only got her out of trouble with the Italian team manager but ended with him making a pass at her, which she deftly evaded, but Gino would in no way be placated; the knowledge that he had been fooled having so injured his masculine pride that he couldn't even accept her apologies. Toni shrugged; win some, lose some, but she was genuinely sorry that she had hurt him, although she knew that he was far too extrovert a character to let it upset him for long.

The other model and the photographer arrived shortly afterwards and later the camera crew, so Toni was immediately involved in trying to carry out her modelling job while at the same time being filmed by the television cameras. They took a great many shots against various backgrounds, both before and during the race, using the back of the photographer's large van as a changing room. The clothes were all thin, floating day and evening dresses, the type of thing rich women would wear to parties and the latest in nightclubs, and completely unsuitable for either the background or outdoor wear, but the photographer was a good one who knew the fashion world, and it certainly wouldn't be the first time that an unusual setting had been used to promote a new style successfully.

Toni's last outfit to be photographed was a black evening dress with a deep plunge neckline and a fairly tight skirt that fell in a series of layers almost to her feet. The bodice, what there was of it, was covered in rainbow layers of coloured sequins, each layer corresponding in colour to sequins sewn on the edge of one of the layers of the skirt. A matching sequin-covered Juliet cap was on her head with her hair fluffed out beneath it, and the make-up woman had given her pearly gold eye-shadow and bright lipstick to carry through the desired effect. It was a striking outfit and one that drew all eyes, but Toni looked at herself critically in a mirror and decided she didn't like it—it was too way out; it was a fun outfit for the wealthy young jet-setter, she supposed.

And of course it had to be this outfit that the director of the television film decided to have her wearing when he did the interview. Toni protested, offering to change into her own clothes, but he said that it would place more of an emphasis on the difference between her two careers if she wore that dress. They found some empty seats in one of the grandstands where the cameras would be able to pick up the race-track in the background and Toni waited rather tensely for the cameras to be set up. This was still a very new experience for her and the first time she had been interviewed directly. And it didn't help a bit when she saw Adam come to watch, leaning his long frame negligently against the back of the stand, arms folded, his eyes studying her coldly.

The interviewer started by asking her the usual questions: how had she got into modelling, to which she answered the truth; and how she had got into motor racing, to which she left out all mention of her father and gave the impression that it was just through her own enthusiasm. There were other questions and then he asked, 'What qualities does a racing driver need to be successful?'

Toni's answer came promptly, 'Basically you have to have a killer instinct, but this has to be controlled and built up into a will to win. You have to have concentration, co-ordination, fast reactions and timing. But the most important driving force is the will to win, to be first across the line.'

'And do you think you have the killer instinct?' the interviewer probed. 'You look far too fragile, especially at the moment.'

Toni smiled thinly. 'I have to have it. I'm competing against men who are far stronger than I am. I need that instinct to carry me through a long race and go the distance. Men have dominated motor racing for far too long, but there are several women entering Formulae racing now.'

Another inevitable question. 'Have you ever crashed?'

'Yes, a couple of times,' Toni acknowledged. 'But I've been very lucky, I've never had anything worse than a few bruises.'

'How about boy-friends?'

Toni laughed. 'Oh, there isn't time for them *and* motor racing.' She glanced up and caught Adam's eyes on her. Her chin came up. 'Men are out—completely!'

CHAPTER FOUR

At the last moment Carinna decided to go with her to Wales, which didn't please Toni very much.

'You'll be bored, there won't be anything for you to do,' Toni warned her. 'I'll be busy testing the car all the time.'

Carinna chuckled. 'You don't really think I'm going down there to keep you company, do you? No, I had a rather more interesting object in mind.'

'Well, if your interesting object is Adam York, you're wasting your time,' Toni told her drily. 'He won't be there.'

'Oh, yes, he will,' Carinna corrected her as she began to pack a suitcase. 'He told me only last night that he expects to get down there for two days at least.'

'He did?' Toni sat down on the bed and frowned crossly. 'What does he want to go down for? *I* certainly don't want him there, he'll just get in the way and start interfering again.' She gave a deep sigh of exasperation. 'Nothing's going right on this darn rally!'

'Oh, don't you think so?' Carinna said smugly. '*I* think it's all going rather well.'

Toni grinned. 'All right, I can see you're dying to tell me. How are you making out with the petty tyrant?'

'He's not like that at all,' Carinna protested. 'Under that cold, hard shell there beats a heart of pure gold, let me tell you.'

'Trust you to find out about the gold,' Toni teased. 'What did he do—give you a present?'

'No, but he has promised to get me an audition as a helper on a television show—you know the sort of thing—you have to look terribly glamorous while you show off the prizes for a quiz game. And if I get that you never know where it might lead,' Carinna added, her eyes lighting up with excitement.

'You'd better be careful,' Toni warned her. 'Soon you'll be getting too good for Adam York and only a millionaire will be able to afford you!'

Carinna made a face and threw a cushion at her. 'Anyway, I'm very grateful to Adam; that's why I'm coming down to Wales with you.'

'So you can demonstrate your gratitude?' Toni asked casually.

Something must have sounded in her voice, because Carinna looked at her quickly. 'You sound as if you'd like to know.'

'Not at all,' Toni said stiffly, and got up off the bed. 'I couldn't care less what you and Adam York get up to. It's entirely your own affair.'

'In every sense of the word,' Carinna agreed. She held up a pair of nylons with a long run in them. 'You know, I think I'll have to open a joint account at the bank—with someone who has lots of money!' she finished drolly.

Toni had to laugh at her. 'Carinna, you're impossible!'

They set off early the next morning and arrived in Wales to find the service crews had arrived before them. The television company had booked them all into a small hotel only a few miles from the test track, and Toni insisted on immediately driving out there with Steve Landors to inspect the car which was waiting for her in a hired workshop. She found one or two things that were not quite to her liking, but on the whole Toni was pleased with the way the car had been adapted; but that was on a purely visual inspection, of course; she would have to wait until she had done a few hundred miles on the test track before she would be completely satisfied.

During the evening Adam telephoned to say that he wouldn't be down until the day after next, which disappointed Carinna and left her with nothing to do the next day except watch while the service crews practised changing the engine, clutch, gearbox, etc. She looked so lost that Toni gave her a stopwatch and a notepad and told her to time the crews and see which one did it quickest, which gave Carinna something to do and introduced a competitive spirit into the proceedings. The men, three of them in each crew, soon settled into well-knit teams and there was friendly, laughing rivalry between them that created a good atmosphere. Three of them, including Steve, were single, and they had to put up with a lot of badinage from their mates about the possible outcome of working with Toni and Carinna.

The girls took it in the harmless way it was meant and spent the evening with them in a local pub, drinking beer and swopping racing experiences. But Toni noticed that Steve, while ready enough to chat with her or the others, didn't have a lot to say to Carinna, who was laughingly flirting with a couple of the married men, although his eyes were often on her even when he was talking to someone else. Not that that was unusual; Carinna was always at her best in a party atmosphere such as this; sparkling, pretty, and full of life, she could guarantee to draw all eyes to her.

The next morning Toni went out with Steve to try

out the car and bed-in the brakes. Toni drove while Steve sat beside her and made notes on any faults she found. They were out for most of the day, and when they got back to the workshop as the late afternoon shadows lay long on the ground, they saw that Adam had arrived and was leaning casually against his Rolls, smoking a cigarette and smiling down at Carinna, who was talking to him animatedly.

When they drew up, he ground out the cigarette and strolled over, his hands in his pockets. 'How's it going.'

Toni remembered their last meeting and deliberately ignored him, slamming the car door and walking away, so it was left to Steve to say, 'Very well, so far, although there are a few things to put right now that we've run the engine in a bit.'

They stood talking together while Toni went into the workshop and sat down at a bench where she began to work out some figures on a piece of paper. Behind her she heard the door open, but she kept her eyes on her work. Someone came up close behind her and she knew it was Adam from the alien tang of his after-shave even before he spoke.

'Sulking, Toni?' he asked in a drawling voice.

She turned to look at him, her face outwardly calm. He was wearing a polo-neck sweater under a soft leather jacket and that, together with his lean features, made him seem different, tougher somehow. She glanced past him, but they were alone, the others were still outside.

'Don't I have reason to be annoyed?' she parried.

'Not unless you can't face up to people knowing what type of girl you are—or acknowledging it yourself,' he added silkily.

Toni flushed with annoyance and came to her feet. 'And just what is *that* supposed to mean?'

'You know as well as I do,' Adam returned coolly. 'You're young and you're beautiful, and you quite deliberately trade on it. You use your sex as a weapon to make people do what you want, to get your own way. And you can switch it on and off like an electric fire—one minute glowing hot, the next cold.'

Toni's cheeks flushed deeper. 'That's ridiculous! You don't know what you're talking about.' But her tone wasn't forceful enough to carry conviction.

'No? What about Gino Moroni? You certainly used him, and nearly lost him his job in the process,' Adam said grimly. 'And you'd have used me too if I hadn't already seen through you.'

'I don't have to take this from you!' Toni swung on her heel and went to walk past him, but Adam caught her arm and swung her round.

'Oh, no, you don't. We're going to get this settled once and for all. I'm not going to spend ten days cooped up in a car with a woman who's sulking like an overgrown schoolgirl.'

'And do you think I want you with me?' Toni burst out angrily. 'I'd rather have anybody but you!'

His lips twisted into a mocking smile. 'Why, because I see through you? Because you can't twist me round your little finger like you can every other man?' A thoughtful look came into his grey eyes. 'And maybe it's a new situation for you at that. You don't like to get into a position where the roles are reversed and someone tries to use you instead. Maybe having a man to master you is just what you need.'

Toni laughed jeeringly. 'And I suppose you think you're the man to do it? Well, let me tell you, Adam

York, there isn't a man alive that I'd let rule me—
especially you!' she added, with loathing in her voice.

But he betrayed no reaction to her outburst other
than a deepening of the mockery in his eyes. 'Good,
I'm glad to hear it. Because I have no intention of wasting my time in sorting out the emotional hang-ups of
a crazy adolescent who's got a chip on her shoulder a
mile wide. Find someone else to take your complexes
out on. All I ask is that you behave like a sensible and
responsible adult for the duration of the rally; after
that you can go to the devil, for all I care,' he added
brutally.

Toni stared at him out of a face gone suddenly pale
with anger. Through teeth clenched tightly together to
stop her losing her temper, she said, 'I am just about
sick and tired of all the inaccurate and—and insane
accusations you keep making about me. *They are totally
unfounded!* All I want to do is to go in for this rally and
do as well in it as I possibly can—even though I have
you in the passenger seat.'

Adam's eyebrows had risen, but he merely answered,
'Well, at least we're both agreed on that. So why don't
we try to call a truce to our—disagreement until the
end of the rally?'

Disagreement? Is that what he thought it? To Toni
it was open war; she'd never met anyone she'd disliked so much in her whole life. But even through her
anger she could see that he was right, there was no
other way if they were to get through the ten days of
the rally.

'All right,' she agreed reluctantly.

'Good. Let's shake on it, shall we?'

To Toni's surprise he took her hand and held it a
moment, his clasp warm and strong. As he did so the

door to the workshop opened and Carinna and Steve came in.

Carinna started to say, 'Haven't you finished yet, Adam, I'm ...' but her voice trailed off.

Toni hastily withdrew her hand and flushed with annoyance. 'We were just shaking hands on a—on a deal,' she stammered, and then wished she hadn't found it necessary to explain when she saw Adam's mouth twist with amusement.

Carinna came up to Adam and put her arm through his. 'I'm starving—and you did promise to take me out to dinner,' she reminded him.

'So I did.' He turned to Steve. 'Is there a decent eating place round here?'

Steve nodded. 'There's an old manor house that's been converted into a restaurant only a few miles away. It's in the Egon Ronay Guide, so it should be good.'

'Then I'll book a table, and I suggest we all go back to the hotel to change and meet in the bar at seven.'

Toni and Steve looked at him and then at each other.

'All four of us?' Steve asked.

Adam looked surprised and Carinna chagrined. 'But of course all four of us,' he said as if he had never thought of anything else.

Toni and Carinna were sharing a room at the hotel, and Carinna, as usual, grabbed the bathroom first but left the door open so that they could talk.

'Toni,' she called plaintively, 'couldn't you persuade Steve to take you out somewhere else—just the two of you?'

'No, I couldn't,' Toni answered firmly. 'Not that I particularly want to play gooseberry with you and Adam, but neither Steve nor I particularly fancy each other.'

'Don't you like him?'

'Oh, sure, he's nice enough.'

There were sounds of splashing as Carinna got out of the bath and then she came into the room with a towel wrapped round her middle. 'I should have thought you two would have hit it off straight away,' she remarked. 'After all, you're both crazy about the same things.'

Drily Toni answered, 'Just because we're both keen on motor racing it doesn't mean that we're going to fall into each other's arms. Besides, he's interested in someone else.'

'You mean he has a girl-friend?'

'No, he's just keen on another girl, but she doesn't reciprocate.'

'Really?' Carinna sounded intrigued. 'Why not?'

Toni went into the bathroom. 'Why so interested—he's hardly your type?'

'No, of course not, but he is sort of attractive, in a big, cuddly-bearish kind of way.' Carinna's voice faded for a few minutes as if she was lost in thought, then she added offhandedly, 'Not that he's at all a marriageable proposition, but that strong, silent type is okay for an occasional date.'

'Speaking of marriage—how are you making out with Adam?' Toni asked as she soaped her left leg. 'Any sign of wedding bells yet?'

Carinna came to lean rather disconsolately against the door jamb. 'No. That's why I had such high hopes of coming down here; I thought I'd be able to get him to myself at last, but now he wants to go out in a four.'

'But you've had him to yourself before, on other dates,' Toni pointed out.

Carinna shook her head ruefully. 'Every time he's

invited me out it's been to a TV show or a party where he's been one of the hosts, so it was always among a crowd or he was busy. We haven't really been out alone together once.' She frowned. 'Honestly, Toni, I don't know what to make of him. Sometimes I think he isn't interested at all, but then he calls me and wants to see me and offers me a wonderful chance like the TV show audition.'

Toni looked at her friend in surprise; she had thought that the affair with Adam had progressed much further, that he and Carinna were getting serious, but if he hadn't even taken her out in a twosome ... And it was unusual for Carinna to be so downhearted over a man, so obviously she must think a lot of him. For a moment Toni wondered if Adam was just stringing her along. It certainly wouldn't be the first time it had happened to either of them, and a flush of anger came to Toni's cheeks. One way and another Adam York was becoming a permanent thorn in the flesh!

She stood up and put on a towelling robe. 'In that case, why don't we encourage him a little?'

Carinna straightened and looked intrigued. 'What do you mean?'

'Maybe I could persuade Steve not to go tonight after all.'

'You will?' Carinna clapped her hands. 'That's great! How?'

'You'll see.' Toni went into the bedroom and picked up the phone. 'Go on,' she urged, 'get your glad rags on—you're going to have a night alone with him at last.'

But it wasn't even midnight before Carinna let herself into their room and found Toni sitting up in bed, poring over some maps.

She looked up. 'Hi. I didn't expect you back so soon.'

Carinna came in and dropped her coat on a chair, then sat on her bed to take off her shoes.

When she didn't answer, Toni said hesitatingly, 'Er — Adam wasn't too annoyed when you told him that Steve and I wanted to try the car out on a night drive, was he?'

Carinna turned towards her. 'I don't know, he didn't say anything about it one way or the other.'

'Oh.' Toni assimilated this, then looked at her friend impatiently. 'Well, how did it go? It was okay, wasn't it?'

Looking at her balefully, Carinna answered shortly, 'No, it wasn't — because he did nothing but ask me questions about *you* the whole time!' And she stormed into the bathroom and slammed the door.

Toni woke early the next morning and quietly dressed in jeans and a thick sweater, trying not to wake Carinna. She left her friend in bed and drove straight to the test-track, not even bothering about breakfast. It was still very early, not yet seven o'clock, and the air was chilly, the weak sunshine of autumn not yet strong enough to dispel the greyness of the morning. The place was still deserted as she parked her car beside the workshop and let herself in. The Escort was just as they had left it the previous night after she and Steve had taken it for a short run to test the lights and realign the headlights. It had taken them only a short time and then they had gone back to the pub to join the other men in the crew; Steve being as keen as she not to have to go out in a foursome and watch Carinna flirting with Adam.

There was an overall hanging from a peg and Toni took it down and put it on, then took a piece of paper that she had been doing some mathematical calculations on from her pocket. She had decided to change the gear ratios of the car and didn't see any point in waiting for someone to come along and do it for her when she could perfectly well do the job herself. Selecting the tools she wanted, Toni lay face upwards on a wheeled board and pushed herself under the car, her legs protruding out of the side.

She had been working contentedly for about twenty minutes, whistling a catchy pop number, when she heard someone come in and saw a pair of male feet walking towards the car. The owner gave one of her own feet a nudge to attract her attention.

Calling, 'Just a minute,' she tightened the last few screws with a spanner and then pushed herself out from under the car, a warm smile of greeting on her face for Steve or whichever member of the crew it happened to be. She caught hold of the side of the car to stop herself as she emerged, then the smile quickly faded as she found herself gazing up at Adam York, towering over her like a giant in Lilliput.

He looked down at her with a sardonic twist to his lips. 'Good morning. Don't tell me you've been working on the car all night? Such devotion is hardly necessary, I assure you.'

Toni went to hoist herself up, but before she could do so, Adam bent and put his hands on her waist, lifting her easily to her feet.

'Thanks, but I can manage.' Quickly she turned away to put the tools back in their boxes.

'You haven't answered my question,' Adam reminded her.

'What? Oh—no, of course I haven't been here all night. I just woke early and decided to come straight here and get on with the job.'

'Why?' His voice was sharp. 'Aren't Steve and the mechanics up to the standard you want? Because, if so, I can always find another crew.'

'Oh, no, it's nothing like that,' Toni hastened to assure him. 'They really know their job and make a good team.' She looked at him earnestly, her eyes troubled. 'Please, Adam, I don't want them changed.' Without thinking, she went to put a hand on his arm to emphasise her point, but then remembered her greasy state and hastily withdrew it.

'Then why you?' he asked brusquely, his voice suddenly cold.

'Because I'm here; I can do the job and so I did it. I am capable of fixing a car as well as driving it, you know.'

'No, I didn't know.'

Her tone impatient, Toni said, 'If I were a man it wouldn't even have entered your head to question my working on the car. When are you going to realise that women are capable of doing anything men can do—and do it better in most cases?' Her eyes sparked a challenge. 'And please don't insult me by making the usual reply that there's *one* thing a woman can never do.'

'Is that the common response you get, then?'

'Yes—usually accompanied by a knowing leer,' Toni retorted sharply.

'Then I think I'd better not make any remark at all, especially with—what was it?—a knowing leer,' Adam replied calmly.

She looked up quickly and saw that he was laughing at her, his eyes amused and crinkled into little laugh lines at the corners, his face so transformed by the smile that for a strange moment she felt as if she'd never really seen him before. She continued to look at him in surprise, then blinked and went to move away, but he said, 'You have a grease mark on your cheek. Here, I'll wipe it off for you.'

He took a clean white handkerchief from his pocket and shook it open.

Toni made a movement of protest. 'There's a rag on the bench.'

But, 'Hold still,' he commanded, and put one hand on her shoulder while he rubbed at her cheek with the other. 'There, that's better. You're presentable again.'

His grey eyes inspected her cheek and then moved across to meet hers. They were standing very close, only a few inches separating them. Toni felt Adam's hand tighten on her shoulder and suddenly felt her heartbeat begin to quicken. The crazy thought came to her that he was going to kiss her. But why he should want to ... and why she wasn't moving away in disgust, instead of standing there, mesmerised almost, her lips slowly parting as his thumb came up to caress her neck ...

'How far did you and Steve go last night?'

His voice grated harshly in her ear. Toni jumped, the spell broken, and quickly turned away, her face flushed.

'What do you mean?' she demanded coldly, putting a hasty interpretation on his unexpected question.

'I meant how many miles did you cover on the night trial, of course.' His tone became derisively sardonic. 'Why, what did you think I meant?'

The colour in Toni's cheeks deepened as she realised that he had been playing with her, leading her on to make a fool of herself. And she had fallen for it too!

'One can never tell—coming from someone like you,' she retorted nastily, adding, 'As a matter of fact we didn't go very far, just enough to assure ourselves that the lights were aligned properly.'

'You could have done it any evening, in fact?'

'Yes, I suppose so,' Toni agreed offhandedly, wiping her hands on a cloth.

'But you chose to do it last night. Why, Toni—so that you wouldn't have to spend the evening in *my* company?' Adam asked. He was leaning against the bench, watching her intently.

She shrugged. 'You suggested we call a truce. The easiest way I know to do that is to have as little to do with the enemy as possible.'

His lips thinned into a mocking smile. 'Scared, Toni?'

Her chin came up. 'Of you? *No way*,' she replied, her voice heavy with derision. 'It was just that I could think of a dozen more interesting ways to spend the evening. And besides,' she looked at him speculatively, 'I was quite sure that you would much rather be alone with Carinna than in a four.'

But his face remained completely impassive, she could read no reaction from it. 'What makes you think that?'

'What makes you think I wouldn't much rather have spent the evening alone with Steve?' she volleyed back in this game of verbal tennis.

For a moment she thought she saw a flicker of something deep in his eyes, but it was quickly gone.

'So I suppose that means you'll be seeing him again tonight?'

'Yes,' she agreed firmly, mentally crossing her fingers

that she would be able to arrange something with Steve.

Drily Adam said, 'All right, just so long as you don't let your emotional entanglements interfere with your rally practice.'

Toni stared at him speechlessly for a few seconds, then said furiously, 'I wasn't *asking* for your permission!'

His eyebrows rose. 'I didn't think you were.' He straightened up. 'What tests have you got planned for the car today?'

Toni glared at him angrily; in some way she couldn't fathom he seemed to have turned the tables so that she felt completely confused, no longer on the attack but on the defensive, like a little girl being talked down to by a grown-up. She bit her lip, trying to think of some crushing retort, but it was too late, he had walked over to the car and was waiting for her to answer his question.

Reluctantly she complied. 'I wanted to try out the intercom system on the crash helmets and also the navigational aids and the two-way radio.'

'Good, as soon as the others get here we'll make a start.'

'We?' Toni asked suspiciously.

'Yes. It's about time I got used to the car. And this will be a good opportunity to get the weight distribution exactly as you want it.'

'That really isn't necessary,' she assured him hastily. 'Steve is near enough your weight and we can ...'

Adam interrupted firmly. 'You can stop arguing, Toni, because I'm going with you today.'

'But you could spend the day with Carinna,' Toni protested cajolingly.

Adam's lips twisted into a wry grimace. 'I came down here on business, not pleasure. Now, which route do you intend to take — through the forest?'

He crossed over to where a large-scale map of the testing area was pinned on the wall, seemingly oblivious of the venomous look Toni shot at him. Even though she disliked Adam she didn't much care for being categorised as merely business either. She would have dearly loved to tell him to go to hell, but she knew that she had no choice but to take him along. Then her eyes lit mischievously; she might have been forced into agreeing to a truce, but that didn't mean that she couldn't make the ride as uncomfortable for him as she could.

Nonchalantly she said, 'No, I've already tried the car out in the forest, I want to take the hill route today.'

As she spoke the metal door to the workshop clanged open and Steve and the other men came in, yawning and discussing the chances of their favourite teams in next Saturday's football games.

Toni explained what she wanted to do and then they loaded the car with all the spare tires and other things they would be carrying on the actual rally. Adam took his seat beside her, fastening himself into the safety straps that resembled a parachute harness and putting on his crash helmet. After a last word with Steve, Toni took her place beside him. Her voice crackled through the intercom that was integrated into the chin-guard of the crash helmet.

'Ready to go?'

'Yes, I'm fine.'

His voice sounded very loud in her ears and Toni reached up to turn down the volume a little. She smiled grimly to herself; well, you won't be feeling quite so fine shortly, she thought with anticipated satisfaction, and started the car to drive out of the workshop.

The route she had chosen had been cut into the sides of a chain of hills. It was narrow, steep and with a great many sharp hairpin bends that had been designed to test a car, and its driver, to the utmost. It wasn't a route for amateurs, especially when it was taken fast, and Toni intended to take it very fast. She wasn't only going to test the car, but Adam York. If he wanted to get into the professional league then he would have to do it the hard way. And if things turned out the way Toni planned, then all that he would prove when she threw the car round the hairpins was that he would be very, very carsick!

The road began to climb up the first of the hills, not yet very steep and with a wide curve at the first bend. Toni took it at a reasonable speed, saving the tricky stuff for the sharper cornering.

'Why don't you try the two-way radio?' she said into the microphone. 'Try Steve's crew first.'

She heard the crackle as he spoke to the vans, which were being driven to points about ten miles away, and then he switched on the intercom again and his voice came back to her over the noise of the engine.

'Steve's van picked it up all right, but there seems to be a fault with the other one; they're looking into it.'

'Fine.' While his attention had been held by the phone, she had leant forward and unobtrusively switched on the heater, boosting it to full power and making sure that all the vents were open.

She drove along through trees and shrubs that bordered their path and saw the road snaking out ahead of her with the first of the sharp hairpins only half a mile or so away. Below them she could see the mist still lingering in the very depths of the valley, a white haze that clung to the ground in a losing battle with the sun and the soft breeze, slowly curling upwards to evaporate in the air. The hills were lush with long grass of a deep emerald green, broken here and there by outcrops of rocks, with an occasional stream of pure mountain water tumbling in a thousand miniature waterfalls to the little river that wound through the valley. The trees were ablaze with colour, each leaf an individual flame of gold, orange and yellow. Many of them had started to fall and were thrown up into the air again with the speed of their passing, dancing and whirling in the slipstream in a last frenzy of life before again coming to rest far behind them.

But Toni had no time now to admire the scenery, she was intent only on humiliating the man beside her. As they neared the bend she said, 'Is the tripmaster registering all right?'

It worked like a charm. Adam bent forward to look down at the instrument as Toni put her foot down hard and went sideways into the hairpin, the engine shrieking a protest as she shoved the stick down through the gears, did a racing change and tore out of the bend and up the hill the other side. Adam was thrown violently sideways and then forward, his helmet banging against the side window but his straps preventing him from hitting the windshield. Having his head down had thrown him completely off balance, as Toni had known it would.

He made a grab for the roll-bar and shot a look at her, but his voice, when he had righted himself, sounded quite calm, if slightly unsteady. 'It seems to be working perfectly. I'll test the map light. Yes, that's okay, too.'

They were coming up to another bend and Toni smiled to herself as she darted a quick glance in Adam's direction and saw him bracing himself to take it. The bends followed in quick succession then, dozens of them, some uphill, some plunging steeply down, and all of them she took at the fastest speed of which the car was capable. And all the time the heater was turning the air inside the car into a hot, dry fug that caught in the throat and made the stomach heave. There was a certain part of this route that drivers nicknamed 'The Slalom' because of the continuous line of S-bends that stretched for over a mile. Toni's smile broadened; if the hairpins and the heat hadn't already made him feel ill, then this would certainly do the trick! She went into the series of loops doing sixty, purposely throwing the car around more than necessary, and waiting in happy anticipation for Adam to desperately yell out to her to stop, unable to stand it any longer.

Only he wasn't calling out. They were halfway through and still he hadn't even groaned. Grimly Toni pressed her foot even harder on the accelerator and then on the brake, swinging the car round in almost cork-screw turns. He must give in soon, he must! She was going too fast to be able to look at him but was sure he must be turning green. Even a fully-experienced navigator couldn't take the punishment she was handing out. But incredibly they were almost at the end of the Slalom and still he hadn't made a murmur. Her teeth gritted in annoyance. Toni raced out of the last bend and into the straight that would lead them down into the valley and back to the workshop.

But the crazy twisting had broken something loose in the trunk, she could hear its metallic rattling even through the thickness of the helmet, which tended to deaden all extraneous noises. Reluctantly she pulled over to the side and stopped.

Adam immediately opened the door and pushed it to its full extent, letting in a gush of clean mountain air. Reaching up, he took off his helmet. Slowly, Toni did the same.

He turned to look at her, showing no discomfort from the rough ride she had given him. Cuttingly he said, 'Nice try, Toni. Can we turn the heater off now—or do you have another pleasant little trick you want to try out on me?'

Slowly Toni leant forward and flipped the switches, not letting him see the unwilling respect in her eyes. She knew very few men who could withstand the sort of treatment she'd put him through. As the buzzing of the booster fan came to a stop it left a sudden silence that seemed somehow louder than all the noise.

To break it, she said hurriedly, 'I'll find out what came adrift in the trunk,' and got quickly out of the car.

They were very high up, almost two thousand feet, and the air felt good after the noxious atmosphere of the car. Toni stopped for a moment to draw deep breaths into her lungs; it felt as heady as pure oxygen. The breeze was strong up here, it caught her hair and pulled it free of the couple of clips she had pushed in the sides to keep it out of her eyes, lifting it up around her head like a silken halo. For a moment she let the wind have its way, enjoying the feel of it in her hair, then she turned and saw that Adam had got out of the car and was leaning against it, with one arm on the roof, watching her. For an instant their glances held until Toni quickly turned away and bent to open the trunk.

Adam came to stand beside her and watched as she restored the jack that had broken loose from its strap.

He didn't attempt to help her, merely taking out a cigarette and lighting it, but even so she was aware of his nearness, and the feeling made her uncomfortable. She shut the trunk with a slam and straightened up to find him looking at her with his usual slightly derisive expression.

'I thought we agreed to call a truce?' he observed mildly.

'Yes, we did,' Toni answered blandly.

'And you don't regard your attempt to make me carsick as breaking that truce?'

Her eyes opened wide in innocent surprise. 'Oh—were you feeling unwell? I was perfectly all right.'

Adam's lips compressed into a thin smile that didn't reach his eyes. 'But then you had the steering-wheel to hold on to.'

Toni returned the smile maliciously. 'Isn't there a saying: "If you can't stand the heat, get out of the kitchen"?'

For an instant there was a sudden menace about him as his mouth tightened into an even thinner smile, but then he nodded towards the exhaust pipe and kicked it with his foot. 'I thought I heard this rattling, it must have come loose as you took one of your gentle curves,' he said sarcastically.

Toni immediately became professionally concerned, getting down on the ground to look. 'I can't see anything, and it's too hot to touch.'

'I'll start up the engine and you can listen for yourself,' Adam offered. 'Keep away from the exhaust fumes—I wouldn't want you to get poisoned,' he added mendaciously.'

Toni stood up, ignoring his sally.

Adam turned on the engine. 'Can you hear it?'

'No,' Toni called back, going down on her hands and knees again at the side of the car. 'Rev it up.'

He did so—and Toni suddenly found herself with a face full of dust and dead leaves as he accelerated and drove away fast down into the valley, leaving her sitting in the road, staring after him in utter disbelief.

CHAPTER FIVE

FOR a full five minutes Toni just sat there, fully expecting him to turn round and come back for her, then she stood up in growing unease, shading her eyes against the sun as she looked expectantly down the road. But all she saw was the Escort, at least two miles away, just disappearing into a piece of woodland in the bottom of the valley. She stared incredulously. How dared he go off and leave her stranded? Rage filled her, as impotent as it was fierce. Furiously she pulled off her driving gloves and threw them on the ground. Damn Adam York! If he thought she was going to walk all the way back to the workshop he was very much mistaken! Why, it must be more than five miles. She found a boulder at the side of the road and sat down on it. She would just wait here until someone came for her.

At first the time went quickly as she thought in loving detail of all the things she'd like to do to Adam: thumbscrews and other torture instruments came into it quite a lot, but did little to lessen her anger. No one had ever *dared* to treat her like this before. Impatiently she looked at her watch. Surely Steve would come for her as soon as he saw that Adam was alone and he found out what had happened. But then she remembered that the two vans were miles away, testing the two-way radios to find out the limits of their range.

She groaned and stood up. Heaven knew when they would get back, and Adam had the car with the other receiver so there was nothing to stop him keeping the vans out for hours if he felt like it. And it was perfectly obvious now that he wasn't going to come back for her, he fully intended to humiliate her by making her walk all the way to the test centre. Picking up her gloves, Toni shoved them into the pocket of her jeans and started along the road, her temper vitriolic.

At first she kept to the tarmac, hoping that someone else might be testing their car and give her a lift, but the road was utterly deserted, the day completely quiet except for the rustle of the wind along the grass and the everlasting song of the birds. Toni stopped to rest and watched a flock of house-martins flying round and round in dizzying circles over her head. Funny, she thought, she couldn't remember the last time she had been alone in the countryside like this, not for years, certainly not since she'd lived in London; life had always been too busy to take time out to watch the birds since then.

The road fell away in a wide, deep curve, and she realised that by cutting across the hillside she could save herself at least a quarter of a mile, so she left the road and took to the open ground, the grass soft and springy beneath her feet. Wild flowers grew everywhere in great profusion; the blue of field scabious fought with the purple of foxgloves and yellow gentians, so many that Toni found it difficult not to step on them. She bent to pick some of the flowers, her thoughts going back, unbidden, to memories of her childhood when they had all gone out for picnics; her mother laughing and beautiful, her father strong and vital, not the dried-up embittered husk that tragedy had turned him into. Toni found a stream and sat down by it, pulling up her knees and resting her chin on them.

For a long time she sat there, her eyes taking in the peace and quiet of the place, but her mind full of tormenting thoughts about her father that were far from tranquil. Never before had she had any real doubts about her ability to carry out her father's wishes, she had been sure that her undoubted skill and tenacity would carry her to the top as he wanted. She only had to keep on racing, keep on winning, and she would eventually be able to drive his car in Formula One races and win his approval at last.

But that drive in Gino's car had altered everything. It had shown her that it needed more than skill and technique, it also needed strength and a reckless, live-or-die kind of courage that she didn't have. Oh, she was brave enough, she knew that, she had to be to take part in racing at all, but it was a bravery based on the knowledge of her own competence in handling a car, not the kind that would take any risk and to hell with the consequences. And that was the only kind that would ever succeed in Grand Prix racing. As for her strength— she could handle cars like the Escort and Formula Fords perfectly well, but, although tall, she was very slender, her weight kept rigorously well under a hundred pounds. Being a model she couldn't afford an ounce of fat or the camera lens would pick it up straight away. And she hadn't been strong enough to control Gino's car at very high speeds, so how on earth would she control her father's turbo-charged job?

Depression sat on her shoulders like a heavy yoke; supposing she let him down yet again and crashed his beloved car? He would have nothing to live for then, nothing to bring that old spark of enthusiasm back into his eyes. For a few minutes she gave way to tears, then resolutely brushed them away. There was always a way round every problem if you looked for it. She would just have to go to weight-training classes to improve the muscles in her arms and shoulders. That would help. And as for the fear—well, she would conquer that too, somehow. But the day was too beautiful to think of that now. Picking up her bunch of flowers, Toni stood up and continued on the long trek back.

As the way descended lower, she could no longer see the cluster of buildings at the centre and decided to stick to the road in case she got lost. Soon she came to the first of the trees where the fallen leaves lay on the ground like a carpet of golden crusty snow and she amused herself by wading through them, kicking the leaves up high into the air for the sheer pleasure of watching them fall again. Her hair had been blown into tangles by the wind and she had unthinkingly pushed a couple of mauve bell-flowers into it above her left ear, accentuating the colour of her eyes in their delicate petals. The wind, too, had brought colour into her cheeks and vitality into her face. She came unhurriedly down the road, enjoying her game, for once uncaring about time.

It was the Escort that caught her eye first. It was parked in a small clearing just off the road so she hadn't noticed it until she was quite close. Toni came to a dead stop in the middle of the road and looked quickly round. Adam was sitting on the ground with his back against a tree trunk, his long legs stretched out and his arms folded on his chest. His eyes were closed and he appeared to be asleep. Got tired of waiting for her, she supposed with a flare of remembered anger. She looked at him speculatively, wondering if he had left the ignition key in the car and whether she could reach it and drive away without waking him. It would give her a great deal of satisfaction to turn the tables on this hateful man. As quietly as possible, she took a couple of tentative steps towards the car, cursing now the leaves that rustled under her feet.

'You're wasting your time.' Adam's voice cut through the stillness and made her jump. 'The key is in my pocket.'

Slowly Toni relaxed, then looked at him undecidedly, wondering whether to teach him a lesson by just ignoring him and keeping on walking, but somehow she had an idea that he wouldn't care either way. And besides, she wasn't used to walking over rough ground and her feet hurt; her stomach, too, was starting to make protesting noises and she remembered that she hadn't bothered with breakfast.

'Cigarette?' Adam took out a packet from his jacket pocket and held it out to her.

Reluctantly Toni crossed over to him and took a cigarette, but to reach the light he held out to her she had to go down on her knees, and then it seemed only sensible to sit down alongside him and share his tree trunk. They smoked in silence for several minutes, but it wasn't a strained silence, strangely enough. And even more strangely, Toni found that she was no longer angry with him for leaving her stranded. She realised, rather unwillingly, that he had paid her back for her own trick very neatly. But neither had worked completely; Adam hadn't succumbed to carsickness, and she hadn't succumbed to the blazing fury he had undoubtedly expected her to show when she saw him again.

As she drew on the cigarette Toni began to wonder why she wasn't angry with him, and at first she thought that it must be because she had walked off her anger, that it had sunk beneath the weight of heavier worries, but after she had mulled it over in her mind a little, she realised that it was because she would have done exactly the same thing in his place—only she wouldn't have stopped and waited, she would have made him walk the whole way back, preferably with the whole crew watching his humiliation. But Adam had waited for her to catch up with him. Did that make him less a vindictive person than she? Reluctantly Toni had to accept that it did.

They had been sitting in silence for quite some time when Adam said casually, 'Do you want to tell me about it?'

Toni shot him a quick glance, but she saw only his profile, strong and firm-jawed, his eyes half shut against the smoke. 'About what?'

'You know perfectly well. About how you came to be such a dedicated man-hater.'

Toni turned away, her face tightening. 'I don't hate *all* men.'

'No,' he admitted, 'you don't hate the ones you can browbeat or who fall for you—you just *despise* those.' He stubbed out his cigarette and, when she didn't answer, reached down to pick up her hand from where it rested on the grass beside him. It was balled into a tight fist. Gently he began to stroke the back of it with his index finger. 'You want to know what I think? I think that somewhere in your past some man played a really dirty trick on you and hurt you so badly that you've been scared to death of trusting a man ever since. Not to mention trying to get your own back on them for all the hurt you suffered.' His finger slid round, forcing its way inside her fist, opening her fingers. 'We're not all swines, Toni.'

'No?' she asked tartly, trying to pull her hand away, but failing. 'How would *you* know?' Pointedly she added, 'How are you making out with Carinna?'

Adam answered quite calmly and without hesitation. 'Carinna isn't interested in me, all she's interested in is what my money and my position can give her.'

Which was such an exact summing-up that it brought Toni up short. She stopped trying to pull away and turned towards him, searching his face. He didn't seem in the least put out.

'If you know that, why keep on seeing her, taking her to parties?' she asked coldly.

'Because I like her, in spite of the fact that she's a little gold-digger, and I'm willing to help her make a career in show business, if that's what she wants.'

'Of course, it couldn't possibly be because of what *you* want from *her*, could it?' Toni asked, her voice heavy with contempt.

Forcefully he answered, 'If by that you mean, am I keeping her sweet in the hope that she'll go to bed with me, then the answer's no. She isn't the type I go for.'

'No? Then just what is your type? You once told me almost exactly the same thing, so that cuts out both blondes and brunettes, which doesn't leave much other than redheads. Are those your type—flame-headed girls with passions to match?' she taunted him.

Adam laughed, a rich masculine sound that sent a squirrel scurrying back up its tree. 'Oh, it isn't a particular look I go for, more the character of a woman; someone soft and feminine who knows how to appreciate what a man has to offer.'

He twined his fingers in hers, his other hand coming up to cover it.

Toni looked down at their entwined hands and from somewhere an imp of devilment rose in her, an urge to try out her powers on this man who had dismissed her so scathingly. It would be very satisfying to bring him to heel, to have him mooning after her like a frustrated tom-cat as so many other men had done in the past, only to realise in the end that she did, in fact, despise them for it. And it would be interesting to see how long Adam could last out—if he did at all.

She came up on her knees and let her hand relax in his. Softly she said, 'Most women can be soft and feminine when a man takes the trouble to make them feel that way.'

He grew still for a moment and then turned quickly to look at her, his eyes speculative. 'Are you saying what I think you're saying?'

Toni brought her eyes into play, looking at him teasingly and making full use of her long lashes. She let her voice become husky. 'What do you think I'm saying, Adam?'

'That you too can be how a woman ought to be? I don't believe it! You're a she-wolf. You devour men for breakfast.'

Toni moved a little nearer so that her knee was touching his thigh. 'You think that because you've always rubbed me the wrong way. Maybe if you'd tried a different approach...' She let her voice drift off suggestively.

Adam leaned his head back against the tree and looked at her through lids half-closed. 'What approach did you have in mind: masterful, insinuating, flattering? I'm open to instruction.'

'Oh, you really can't expect me to tell you something like that,' Toni returned, smiling a little and making full play with her eyes now, openly flirting and feeling more sure of him every minute, certain that he must be intrigued by her sudden volte-face. 'You'll just have to find out for yourself.'

'But what if I never hit the jackpot? I might never find out if you can really be feminine and soft and sweet.'

Putting a hand on his shoulder, Toni looked at him as softly as she knew how. 'Oh, I assure you, I can be everything you've ever wanted in a woman,' she breathed.

'You wouldn't like to prove that last statement, would you?' Adam asked, his voice openly inviting.

Hiding the gleam of triumph that came into her eyes, Toni eased herself round until she was sitting on his lap, then lifted her hands one each side of his face. Lips parted sensuously, she bent forward and began to explore his mouth in little kisses that brushed his lips tantalisingly, promising everything but giving nothing. She moved deeper into his lap, leaning her body against his, expecting him to put his arms round her, to take the initiative from her and to kiss her, and by so doing fall into the trap she had set for him. But his arms stayed by his sides and he let her make all the running. Incensed, Toni let her fingers play in the silky hairs at the back of his neck, her body writhe against his, while her kiss became deeper, more passionate.

She thought she felt a shudder run through him then and moved in for the kill, but something made her look at him under her lashes and she became suddenly still. Adam had his eyes fully open, watching her steadily. Toni blinked; she'd never known anyone who kissed with their eyes open before. She went to go on kissing him, then stopped. Slowly she lifted her head.

There was nothing in his eyes except perhaps sardonic amusement, certainly not passion or even lust, none of the emotions that should have been there after her little performance, that had always been there whenever she'd tried it before. Not that she had ever had to go quite as far as that to get the desired effect.

Quickly now, she pushed herself away from him and got to her feet, trembling for no apparent reason and feeling uncharacteristically ashamed. Adam, too, stood up, brushing the leaves from his trousers.

'I guess you saw through that one too?' Toni said tightly.

He nodded. 'It was rather obvious.'

A rush of colour came to Toni's cheeks. Waspishly she snapped, 'And I suppose I should have realised that you can't arouse emotion in a lump of stone!'

Something flickered in Adam's eyes. He caught her arm and swung her round to face him. 'When the day comes that I feel like kissing you, then you'll *know* that you've been kissed!'

Toni stared at him for a moment, then hastily swung away and walked towards the car. Adam followed at a more leisurely pace. Going round to the other side of the car, he said, 'You still haven't answered my question.'

She looked at him across the roof. 'What question?'

'I asked you why you hated men.'

The flush deepened and she bent to get into the car. 'The key, please,' she snapped out as soon as he got in beside her.

He fished in his pocket for it and held it out to her, dangling it between his fingers. 'You're going to have to tell me sooner or later, you know, so why not now?'

Toni snatched the key from him, fumbling in her

haste to insert it into the ignition.

'Oh, and by the way,' Adam added nonchalantly, 'whenever you want to try that last trick again I'd advise you not to make it quite so sudden. Try a longer lead-up to it next time, it would make it more convincing.'

The fragile hold on Toni's temper snapped completely. 'You pig! You skunk! You're laughing at me! Why, I'd like to . . .' Her fist came up to punch him, but Adam caught it neatly as he burst into laughter. 'Damn you, Adam York! God, how I hate you!' she yelled at him. But to her fury he continued to shake with laughter as she tried ineffectively to hit him.

They arrived back at the workshop almost at the same time as the vans and Toni immediately slammed out of the car to go across and talk to Steve. To her surprise she saw him helping Carinna out of the passenger seat.

'Hi. When did they pick you up?'

'I saw Steve driving past the hotel and got him to take me along,' Carinna explained. 'You don't mind, do you?'

'No, of course not. I just hope you weren't too bored. Adam and I were the only ones who were doing anything interesting this morning,' Toni added, then flushed as she realised that Adam had strolled up behind her and would undoubtedly read a different interpretation into that remark. 'What I mean is, the vans were only trying out the two-way radios,' she added hurriedly.

'Oh, that's all right, I quite enjoyed being chauffeured round the countryside,' Carinna assured her.

'Did you manage to trace the fault in the fuel system?' Steve asked.

Toni looked blank, but Adam said smoothly, 'Yes,

it's fine now; took a while to find it though.' And she realised that he had, over the radio, given it as an excuse for the time he had been waiting for her. It had never even occurred to her that the crews would have wondered what happened to them.

She shot a fulminating glance at Adam and drew Steve aside. 'Steve, we're going to have to work out exactly how much gas we need for each stage and take just that amount plus a gallon for a safety margin. The car handles much better without the weight of a full tank.'

Their talk became technical as they strolled into the workshop leaving Adam and Carinna together. The other men had already got out their flasks of coffee and sandwiches that they had brought with them from the hotel and were sitting on some benches at the end of the workshop. Steve collected his lunch bag and went to join them, but Toni hesitated, looking towards the door, anxious about Carinna. Now that she knew Adam definitely wasn't interested in her friend, she must find an opportunity to tell Carinna as soon as possible. Toni didn't want her to go on fooling herself about Adam a minute longer than necessary.

As she hovered uncertainly, the door opened again and they both came in, Carinna looking up at Adam and laughing, while Adam had his arm round her waist, giving her the full force of his charm. As they came towards them Adam looked up and caught Toni watching them. In answer to the venomous glower she darted at him he merely gave a slow, mocking grin and playfully picked Carinna up and lifted her over one of the benches so that she gave a squeal of pretended fright mixed with laughter.

Toni took her place on a bench as far away from

them as possible. The sooner she got Carinna on her own and told her the truth, the better. A thought struck her as she lifted a sandwich half-way to her mouth: or did that narcissistic devil think that Carinna wouldn't believe her and would want to go on seeing him? Automatically she bit into the sandwich and almost choked on her food. The rotten, hateful ... She began to cough and the man next to her had to thump her on the back. Gaspingly she blinked eyes that had begun to water and the first thing that came into focus was Adam watching her with a look of false sympathy.

'Bitten off more than you can chew, Toni?' he asked mockingly.

Any hope Toni had of getting Carinna by herself was dashed when the film team arrived shortly after lunch and wanted to get to work immediately. Two of them went out with her in the car and filmed her as they drove along and then they wanted her in the shot as they filmed Adam talking about the navigational instruments they had incorporated into the Escort. Before today Toni had been certain that he would fall down here, that his amateurishness would stand out like a sore thumb, but after that ride this morning she was no longer so sure. And of course he sailed through the interview, explaining each gadget knowledgeably and succinctly, without having to refer to her once. Toni listened to him in growing perplexity; either he had done his homework very well or else he was a far more experienced rally competitor than she had supposed. She made a mental note to phone her father and ask him to go through as many old rally reports as he could find and see if he could come across Adam's name in any of them.

By the time they had finished it was getting late, and

instead of going straight back to the hotel they all drove into the nearest town for a meal, and then someone mentioned that there was a classic film on at the local cinema and suggested they go on there. Toni opened her mouth to refuse, but Carinna leapt at the idea. She also noticed a challenging look in Adam's eyes, so she hastily changed her mind and went along with them, still hoping for an opportunity to speak to her friend alone, but to her chagrin, Toni somehow found herself seated between Adam and the film director, while Carinna was further along the row next to Steve. She stood up to change seats, but Adam pulled her down again.

'Sit down and behave yourself like a good little girl and I might buy you an ice lolly in the interval,' he told her outrageously.

Toni glared at him and would dearly have loved to tell him just exactly what he could do with his rotten lolly! At first she watched the programme in a fulminating silence, but as the main feature progressed she began to lose herself in it. It was a love story and terribly sad. Toni groped in her bag for a handkerchief, but unable to find one she surreptitiously lifted a finger to wipe away a tear and sniffed a little. The next moment a man-size handkerchief was thrust into her hand.

'Here,' Adam said. 'Use this.'

She accepted it gratefully, too lost in the film to care where it came from, and it was only when the epic was over and the lights came on again that she realised to her acute embarrassment that Adam had heard her being a maudlin fool over a film of all things! So now he had another weapon to taunt her with. After the film they drove back to the hotel in a convoy of cars, but mercifully she managed to get into a different one from Adam, but at the hotel they all gathered again in the bar for a farewell drink with the film crew who would be leaving very early in the morning, and Toni waited in acute discomfort for Adam to make some derisive remark about her lapse to the others, to invite them to laugh at her. But strangely he made no reference to it whatsoever, not even to ask for his handkerchief back. Toni found herself watching him in growing puzzlement. If he had given her a similar opportunity she would have made full use of it as a means of exercising her wit on him and holding him up to ridicule. She set down her glass with a snap and leant back in her chair. Damn Adam York! Why didn't he ever do what she expected him to?

It was nearly midnight before she and Carinna were at last alone together in their room and Toni shut the door behind them with a feeling of relief mixed with nervousness as she wondered how Carinna would take it.

'Look, you'd better sit down a minute. I've got something to tell you,' she began awkwardly as her friend took off her coat.

'You sound terribly serious,' Carinna answered cheerfully, kicking off her shoes and lying back on the bed. 'What is it? Are you going to tell me that I'm getting in your way and I've got to go home?'

'No, of course not, you know I'm pleased that you came along.' Toni hesitated. 'No, it's about Adam. We —that is *he* talked about you when we were out this morning. And he admitted that—well, that he likes you but he has no emotional interest in you.'

'I don't turn him on, is that what you're trying to say?' Carinna asked bluntly.

'Well, yes. And he also said that he'd—er—realised

what game you were playing.'

'You mean he's seen through me?'

'Yes, I'm afraid so,' Toni admitted. 'Sorry, love.'

'You needn't be. I already knew all that.' Carinna swung her long legs off the bed and stood up.

Toni gazed at her in surprise. 'You did? How?'

Carinna paused at the bathroom door to look back at her. 'Because Adam told me, of course.'

'*He told you?*' Toni's eyes opened wide in amazement. 'When did he tell you?' She raised her voice to call through the door as Carinna shut it. 'Hey, when did he tell you?'

Carinna opened the door again and poked her head round. 'All right, you don't have to shout! He told me last night, of course, when he took me out to dinner. He said that he enjoyed my company and hoped we'd remain friends, but as far as he was concerned that was as far as it went.'

'So he'd already told you before he ... Did he ...' Toni went to ask another question, her eyes alight with interest, but Carinna shut the door firmly in her face and left her to her own thoughts.

Slowly Toni undressed, her mind working on the interesting piece of information Carinna had given her. She wondered why Adam had chosen last night to tell her friend; because he realised Carinna had come to Wales just to be near him and he didn't want her to have any ideas about getting serious, she supposed. Which was quite a gentlemanly thing to do, and what some might consider to be more than Carinna deserved. Except that Toni was fiercely loyal to her friend and didn't think anything of the kind. And besides, there wasn't an ounce of harm in Carinna, all she wanted was a rich husband, an ambition shared by most unmarried girls the world over. And being young and beautiful, Carinna had much to offer in return, so Toni didn't consider her to be a gold-digger at all, merely ambitious.

When they were both in bed, she hesitated before putting out the light and looked across at Carinna, who was putting cream on her face.

'If you don't want to stay on here till the end of the week now, I'm sure the film crew would give you a lift back to London in the morning.'

Carinna lifted her chin to massage the cream into her neck. 'I might as well stay until you leave; I'm not likely to get any modelling assignments at such short notice. And anyway, I could do with a few more days' holiday and it's quite restful here.'

Toni looked at her with misgivings. 'You're not hoping you can make Adam change his mind, are you? Because I'm sure he won't.'

Carinna looked at her and laughed. 'No, of course not. I haven't *that* high an opinion of my charms. And Adam is quite definitely the type who makes a decision and sticks to it. You've realised that for yourself, surely?'

'Yes, of course I have.' The look Toni gave her was a little piqued. 'You don't seem very upset about it?'

Yawning, Carinna snuggled down in bed. 'I'm not, funnily enough. I suppose it was because Adam gave me the brush-off so nicely and seems to mean it that he still wants to be a friend. Usually they try and bribe, blackmail or coerce you into bed before they drop you. And let's face it—platonic men friends are few and far between and should be hoarded like gold-dust!'

Casually Toni asked, 'He didn't, then—proposition you?'

'No, nosey, he didn't. I never even had to fight him off. And now can we please put the light out and go to sleep? I'm tired.'

'Oh, sorry.' Toni pressed the switch on her bedside lamp and lay back on her pillows, but somehow she didn't feel at all sleepy. She tried to concentrate on the trial run she would be putting the car through tomorrow, but her thoughts kept slipping back to Adam York. She wondered if he was immune to Carinna because he already had a girl-friend, but in that case why had he bothered to take her out at all? It was all very puzzling. For a moment she let her imagination conjure up a picture of what Adam's ideal girl would be like. Some long-haired creature who wore chiffon and lace, who called him darling all the time and who let him treat her like a doormat, she supposed. Toni made a face in the darkness. Yeuk! Still, they say you always got what you deserved, and Adam certainly didn't deserve anything better, she thought with some satisfaction.

But then she remembered other incidents that had happened that day and the reluctant respect came back. Oh, dear, she hoped he wasn't going to turn out to be nice after all, someone she ought to be polite to, because she would much, much rather go on hating him. Then a question occurred to her that she had been wanting to ask all day.

'Carinna,' she said urgently, 'are you awake?'

A groan came from the other bed. 'How can I be anything else when you keep talking to me? What is it now?'

'Last night you said that Adam asked you questions about me—what did he want to know?'

'Oh, no, do we have to go into that now? Why can't it wait till the morning?'

'There won't be time tomorrow,' Toni answered impatiently. 'Come on, Carinna—give!'

'Oh, all right, I suppose I won't get any peace unless I tell you,' the other girl sighed. 'Well, let's see—it didn't start as an outright catechism; the conversation just sort of got round to you, if you know what I mean. First we were talking about the television audition and he asked me how I got into modelling, and then he wanted to know if we worked together very much. Yes, that's how you came into it.'

'Yes, well—what else did he want to know?'

'Don't rush me, I'm trying to think,' Carinna grumbled. 'I think then he asked how you got into motor-racing.'

'Lord, you didn't tell him about my father, did you?' Toni asked aghast.

'No, of course I didn't. You're so darn uptight and sensitive about it that I wouldn't dare. I just told him what you always tell people.'

'Thank heavens! What did he ask next?'

Confidently Carinna said, 'Oh, I remember that: he didn't come right out with it, he was very subtle, but he tried to find out if you'd ever had a serious relationship with anyone—been engaged or lived with a man, that sort of hot affair.'

'What did you tell him?' The question came out in rather a strangled tone.

'Well, now ... what *did* I tell him?' Carinna murmured musingly. 'It's so difficult to remember.'

'Carinna, will you please stop teasing and get on with it?' Toni said threateningly.

'All right—but only if you let me borrow your new

black suit when I go for my audition.'

Toni hesitated for only a few seconds before she capitulated. 'Oh—all right. Now, what did you say?'

Smugly, Carinna answered, 'I told him that if he wanted to know the secrets of your no doubt murky past, he'd just have to ask you himself! And now I'm going to sleep and I'm not going to say another word —except thanks for the loan of the suit!' she finished triumphantly.

Toni laughed. 'I would have lent it to you anyway. Not that you deserve it.'

She settled down in bed again and stared into the darkness. So Adam had been trying to probe into her past, had he? And not only behind her back, he had even taken Carinna's advice and come right out and asked her himself why she was a man-hater. Toni smiled rather grimly; it was ironical really how he had leapt to the conclusion that she must have had an unhappy love affair when she'd never even had a steady boy-friend in her life! Oh, she'd dated lots of men over the years, dozens of them, but she'd always dropped them the minute they began to get serious. Nothing must be allowed to come between her and motor-racing. She must fulfil her father's ambitions first, and when he was appeased—well, then perhaps there might be time to start living for herself, even to hope to find someone she could respect, a companion she wouldn't mind sharing her life with. But as for love—she almost laughed aloud—that was for the birds. Just something people wrote about in songs and films, and that happened to other people—sometimes.

Scenes from the film she had seen that night came flooding back, and suddenly she was filled with an intense feeling of frustration and longing that was like a physical torment. It was raw and uncontrolled and so violent that she bit into her pillow to stop herself from moaning aloud. She lay there, fingers clenched, trying to pull herself together, willing herself to control her emotions. But never before had she experienced anything like this. Okay, she had felt frustrated lots of times in the past, both mentally and physically, but she had always been able to get in the car and go for a drive, or worked it off in some other way—going out and buying some new clothes was the favourite therapy, but they had been only negligible compared to this. This hurt.

But gradually she overcame it by becoming angry with herself for letting her emotions run away with her. And because it is against human nature to be angry with oneself for long, she turned her annoyance on to the nearest convenient object, which was, of course, Adam York. So he had dared to go prying into her affairs behind her back, had he? she thought resentfully, conveniently forgetting that he had also faced her with it. Well, truce or no truce, she had every intention of making him regret every minute he had to spend in her company. And eventually she fell asleep still working out as many ways as possible of making his life unbearable.

Regrettably, however, Toni had no chance to put these in operation, because she and Adam had only covered a few miles in the car the next morning when there was a short in the electrical system which burnt out some of the wiring and they had no choice but to send for the service vans.

They towed the car back to the workshop and after only a brief inspection Steve said ruefully, 'I'm afraid it's a full day's job; we'll have to strip the melted wires out and replace them completely.'

Adam stood listening, hands in his pockets. 'In that case there's no point in my hanging around; I have to be back in London tomorrow anyway.' He turned to Toni. 'Perhaps we can arrange to take the car out again somewhere nearer London before the rally starts?'

'That really won't be necessary,' she told him with a smile as sweet as her tone was acid. 'Another day's practice with *you* isn't going to make the slightest bit of difference. There's no need for us to meet again until we have to check in at the start of the race. If I need anything in the meantime, I'll inform your secretary,' she added coldly.

Adam's jaw tightened for a moment, but he said mildly enough, 'You're forgetting that we have to compare the open stages we've been given with the area maps, work out our pace notes and that sort of thing.'

Her smile deepening, Toni looked at him in open amusement. 'Why, Adam,' she said silkily, 'where did you learn all that rallying jargon? It does help to give an impression of experience if one can pick up the right words, doesn't it? But please don't worry your head about anything like that, I wouldn't want to burden you with technicalities.' Her eyes cold, she pushed home the final knife-thrust. 'Just leave it to the professionals who understand these things.' And she turned and walked nonchalantly away, forcing herself not to turn round to see how he had taken it.

CHAPTER SIX

THE early morning light at Brands Hatch on the first day of the R.C.C. Rally was not bright enough for the dozens of overalled mechanics who swarmed over the competition cars like bees round a hundred honeypots in the pits complex, everywhere there were extra, powerful electric floodlights set up as well as hand-held lamps that the mechanics used to see into the furthermost depths of engines and gearboxes. The noise was deafening; the roar of revved-up engines, the shouts of instruction or excited anger, the clanging of a car transporter delivering a set of team cars and service vehicle. And over everything the strong smells of gas and oil that seemed to act as some kind of stimulant to all motoring enthusiasts the world over.

Toni stood in the middle of it all and was just as full of nervous exhilaration as anyone. It hung in the air like a radium cloud, an intense atmosphere of heady anticipation and almost frenzied excitement that made everyone shout and laugh louder than was necessary, that made the mechanics double-check something that they knew was already perfect. Even Steve, who usually kept his cool in any crisis, had become infected by it and had just blown his top because one of the crewmen had neglected to put a spanner back in exactly the right place in the tool-box. Toni smiled to herself; they were all fussing around the Escort like a lot of flustered hens with only one chick, and taking absolutely no notice of her at all — she might just as well have not been there.

But she had been unable to stay away and try to snatch another hour of sleep as she had been advised to after checking in at the organisers' office with all her relevant documents and papers. The excitement had been too great, and besides, she had slept almost solidly the previous day, with the help of some sleeping pills, and she now felt wide awake and agog to start. And this time between checking-in and waiting for the scrutineer to come and look the car over and pass it ready to take part was one of the times she liked best; there was none of the mental and physical exhaustion that would inevitably come later to clog her senses; she was tinglingly aware of everything around her: the bustling activity, the noise, the smells, the cold November air that crept inside her clothes but was as nothing to the fever-heat of anticipation.

She looked at the car and felt a surge of pride; its paintwork, a bright shiny red, had been lovingly polished, but was now almost obscured by stickers showing her competition number—number thirty-two—the sponsor's name and of course her own name and emblems from all the notable wins she had had in the past. It looked well worth all the time and trouble that had gone into it: the week in Wales, all Steve's hard work getting the balance and motorised parts exactly right, the two weeks that she had spent alone in her own sports car, doing a run over the route—a reconnaissance tour that led all the way to Scotland over the parts of the open stages that she was able to cover. The secret stages of course no one yet knew, and some of the other parts, in the Forestry Commission and stately home sections for instance, wouldn't be opened until the rally itself, and so would be completely new to her. Normally Toni wouldn't have worried too much about that, relying on her navigator to guide her through, but she had so little faith in Adam's capabilities that she had spent days learning the map directions almost off by heart—there was no time to stop and check your map references in the middle of a rally stage! She had remembered to ask her father to check back through the records for any mention of Adam's name, but he had gone through the list of navigators in British rallying for the last five years and there had been no trace of him. So she was on her own, with Adam just dead-weight in the passenger seat—luckily a passenger who didn't get carsick, but that was about all she could say for him.

Toni gave a little sigh, feeling suddenly despondent despite her nervous excitement. She had determinedly tried to push all thoughts of Adam York out of her mind during the weeks since she had last seen him in Wales and had succeeded to a great extent, but, strangely, when he did come to mind it was never in connection with the rally but always as an unbidden recollection of that nasty little scene when she had tried to seduce him and had failed so miserably. The words he had spoken then echoed in her mind now: 'When I decide to kiss you, you'll know that you've been kissed.' Not if, but when. Toni shivered suddenly and tried to pull herself together, shaking off the strange, empty feeling that filled her. She looked up to see how the men were progressing—and saw Adam only a short distance away, walking purposefully towards her. She hadn't expected to see him, his presence wasn't necessary on the first day of the rally, and the unexpectedness, together with the fact that she had just been thinking of him, made her vulnerable.

Her eyes widened and her lips parted a little in surprise. Adam came straight to her, his grey eyes holding hers as he looked at her intently. Toni felt a sudden surge of emotion that made her start to tremble. Her face paled and she tried to look away, but Adam said softly, 'Hallo, Toni,' and held out his hand towards her.

Automatically Toni put her hand in his, but he didn't shake it, just held it tightly in his, his grip warm and strong. It reminded her vividly of when he had taken her hand as they sat under the tree together and to what it had led. Hastily she snatched her hand away, her cheeks flushed with colour now.

Stiffly she said, 'You needn't have come today, you know. We're only doing the Mickey Mouse stages and I don't need a navigator for that.'

Adam's left eyebrow rose questioningly. 'Mickey Mouse stages?'

Steve came over to join them and nodded to Adam. 'She means that on the first day they always have all the fancy driving stuff—it's just showing off for the benefit of the crowds of spectators really, not proper rallying at all.'

'I see.' Adam turned to Toni and smiled. 'Evidently I don't know all the jargon after all.' When she didn't reply he added in a more businesslike tone, 'Have you checked in yet?'

She nodded shortly. 'Yes, an hour ago.'

'Oughtn't you to be getting some sleep, then?'

Toni frowned. 'Not that it's any concern of yours, but no,' she told him hostilely.

Steve hastily intervened as the vision of his two principals having a blazing row even before the rally started appeared to become more than a possibility. 'Toni wants to be here when the scrutineer comes round. Most of the drivers do it,' he said conciliatingly.

He drew Adam over to the car and began to talk to him out of her hearing. Toni looked across at them moodily, all the anticipation and excitement of the day suddenly gone like a burnt-out rocket. Why did he have to come today? The next nine days were going to be long enough without adding the first day, the best day of all to them. And she had immediately felt so antagonistic towards him—well, no, not quite immediately, for the first couple of minutes she hadn't known quite how she felt, but her emotions had soon crystallised into the anger and resentment he always seemed to rouse in her. She gave a vague, almost despairing little shake of her head, wondering just what she'd done to deserve having someone to whom she was so fundamentally incompatible as her co-driver.

They had to wait nearly an hour for the scrutineer to reach them, during which time Toni wandered off to compare notes with the other women drivers in the rally. There were five of them altogether this year, which was better than they had ever done before, but only one woman had the advantage of having taken part in a previous year. She generously gave them one or two tips, but had the usual grouse about not being taken seriously by the male competitors. But they all agreed that if more women kept entering motor racing *and* being successful, then the men would just *have* to sit up and take notice.

Toni hovered anxiously as the scrutineer checked over the car, but she knew that she needn't really have worried; Steve and his men had done such a marvellous job on it that the official hadn't even the slightest criticism to make. As soon as the scrutineer had passed it, Toni had to drive the car into a parc-fermé, a sealed-off car park, and leave it there until all the cars had been passed as roadworthy and the rally could start.

As Toni walked back to the pits she pulled the collar of her parka closer round her neck. The weather was unusually cold for November, there had been a ground frost in the night and the roads had been slippery as they drove there this morning. She hoped it was only a freak low in the atmosphere and would clear up quickly, because as the rally progressed north towards Scotland the air was bound to become colder, which could mean snow on the high ground. And that could be tricky when you were trying to drive round winding mountain roads at seventy miles per hour!

Some spectators had started to arrive already, all of them muffled up in boots, thick coats and scarves. A majority of men and boys of course, most motoring enthusiasts were, but here and there Toni noticed the more brightly-coloured parkas and woollen hats of a few women who had been keen enough to brave the cold. Or had come along simply because they wanted to be with their husbands or boy-friends, she thought wryly, then grinned to herself: greater love hath no woman than to stand in the freezing cold all day watching a sport she couldn't care less about!

Thanks to all the media coverage that she had already been given, Toni's face had become known to a great many people, especially motor-rallying supporters, and as she walked along she overheard several people pointing her out to their companions, and one youth even came up and asked her for her autograph. It was the first time it had ever happened to her and Toni felt acutely embarrassed and so nervous that her signature ended up as a hopeless squiggle. But the boy seemed pleased enough and thanked her profusely that she hurried away in even greater embarrassment.

Adam was standing near the entrance to the pits and eyed her keenly as she came up to him, noting her flushed cheeks and the way she was hurrying. When she went to go past him he reached out and held her arm. 'What is it?' he asked sharply. 'I saw someone come up to you. Did he upset you—insult you in some way?'

His jaw thrust forward aggressively and his eyes darted over to where the youth was walking back to his place in the stands. Hastily Toni answered, 'Oh, no, it was nothing like that.' Her blush deepened as she added rather dazedly, 'He—he asked me for my autograph.'

Adam's eyes came quickly back to her face and he murmured almost under his breath, 'Well, I'll be ... Haven't you ever been asked for it before?'

Toni shook her head, and because she was still unnerved, added confidingly, 'I'm afraid I made an awful mess of it.'

He began to smile and suddenly Toni realised how stupidly naïve she must have sounded. Angry with herself, she said snappishly, 'Anyway, it's no business of yours even if he had accosted me; I'm quite capable of fighting my own battles, thank you very much!'

The mocking expression back on his face, Adam said, 'Ah, yes, motor-racing's own iron lady. So tough that being asked for your autograph throws you into utter confusion.'

Toni's face set grimly. 'Not so confused that I can't tell you to go to hell!' she returned fiercely.

She went to move away, but he tightened his hold on her arm. Softly, menacingly, he said, 'One day, young lady, you are going to go just a little bit too far, and I won't be answerable for the consequences.'

Toni turned round to let fly at him angrily, but found his eyes looking steadily into hers only a few inches away. The words died in her throat as she stared at him for a long moment, her thoughts in turmoil. Eventually she managed to say rather unsteadily, 'Is that supposed to be some sort of threat? Because, if so, it doesn't frighten me one little bit.' She tried to say it jeeringly, but even to her own ears her tone lacked conviction.

Quickly, then, she moved away from him and walked towards Steve, but to her annoyance found that she was shaking. Sternly she told herself it was because of the race; why else should she feel so tense and nervous? And yet something made her look back at Adam, only to feel a cold surge of what felt strangely like disappointment when she saw that he had gone.

Together with Steve and the other mechanics, Toni went for a quick coffee and sandwich, but this was cut short by the arrival of the Century Vision film crew who wanted to do a last interview before the rally started. With them they brought a sheaf of telegrams they had received wishing her luck and also a toy hippopotamus in bright green fur.

'We noticed you didn't have a mascot,' the director told her, 'so we brought this along for you to put in the car.'

Toni laughed at the cute toy and gave them each a kiss on the cheek by way of thanks, but said, 'He's lovely, and I really appreciate the thought, but I wonder if you'd mind if he rode in one of the service vans instead? You see, I don't usually carry a mascot, because if you ever forget it then you start worrying about what might happen and you lose your concentration.'

And as it proved she had no need of any good luck charm that day, because she did really well in all the driving skill stages and by the end of the day was lying sixth in her class. The racing tires that Steve had fitted on the car gripped the ground beautifully even though the temperature was still below freezing, but they took it out on her arm and leg muscles. By the end of that day's stages, the tendons in her wrists ached so much that she could hardly grip the steering-wheel, and she gave a shuddering sigh of relief when she was able to relax at last.

All the entries had come through the first day unscathed; it was only as the rally progressed further up the country and the conditions become tougher that the cars would start to fall out either through accidents or mechanical trouble, leaving only the best cars and the best drivers in the competition. Luck came into it, of course, as it must come into everything one does, but Toni held the firm belief that if the car was mechanically sound, the back-up teams properly organised, and most of all the driver always on the alert and concentrating on the job, then only a completely chance calamity could stop you from completing the course. Usually it is the driver who makes the fewest mistakes who wins.

As soon as the stages were over, Toni handed the Escort over to Steve to change the racing tires for rough-road ones and to service it ready for the long drive up the motorway, while she fell into bed at a nearby hotel for the few hours' rest she would be permitted before it was time to set off again.

When she got back to the course she found the car ready and waiting for her, its engine warmed up, the ice melted off the windows, the tires changed. Adam, too, was waiting, wearing what looked like a black ski-suit open at the neck to reveal a thick sweater underneath. Toni nodded to him but concentrated on talking to Steve who got in touch with the other service van over the radio to check that they were safely on their way to the first service point half-way up the motorway.

When there was nothing else that she could possibly think of to check, Toni looked at her watch and then turned reluctantly to Adam who had been standing nearby quietly smoking a cigarette.

'Well, I suppose we'd better get in the car.'

He merely nodded and ground out his cigarette, his expression completely unreadable, but Toni felt a flash of temper, sure that he was inwardly laughing at her because he knew that she had been trying to hang it out until the very last minute before she had to give in to the inevitable moment when she would have to take her seat beside him, the seat she would have to occupy for the next nine days and nights!

Toni settled herself into the driving seat that had been custom-made to fit her, buckled herself into the seat harness that went across her lap, over her shoulders and into the head rest, and put the astronaut-like crash helmet with its chin guard and her name painted on it, over her head. Beside her Adam was doing the same, but also stowing into the side pockets his clip-board with their precious road-book, the document on which the marshals would enter their time at the start and finish of every stage. The route card and maps he also put in special pockets well within his reach, not that he would need them much if Toni remembered the route correctly.

Adam's voice sounded loudly in her ears. 'We'd

better test the intercom. Can you hear me okay?'

'Yes, perfectly. You?'

'Coming through loud and clear.' Even over the inter
com she could hear the mockery in his voice.

It occurred to her then that this whole thing was just
a joke to him, an amusing interlude from which he
would get some publicity and perhaps an amusing
anecdote to tell over dinner. She couldn't for the life
of her see what else there could possibly be in it for
him.

The cars were leaving at one-minute intervals, their
headlights blazing as they prepared to drive through the
night, the throaty exhausts of a hundred cars sending up
clouds of carbon monoxide vapour into the freezing
darkness. Steve put his head through the window and
shouted, 'Goodbye. Good luck!' and then they were
moving forward to take their place in the line. Luckily
they weren't too far back in the line, although the first
competitors would be half an hour ahead of them before
they even left Brands Hatch.

Now there were only a couple of cars in front of them.
They had been sitting silently, each absorbed in their
own thoughts, Toni swallowed up in the feverish excitement she always felt at this point in a rally. She turned
her head to look at Adam—glancing sideways was difficult with the helmet on—and suddenly she found herself
saying, 'Just *why* are you here? Why did you want to
take part in the rally?'

He, too, turned his head, his eyes somehow seeming
more withdrawn and enigmatic through the visor. 'Because I wanted to be alone with you, of course.'

Toni's eyes blazed at him furiously. She jumped the
car forward to the starting line while the marshal
marked their road book, and rammed the throttle down

the second he started to lower his arm to signal them away.

As they moved off, despite her anger, Toni automatically reached out to set the electronic tripmeter which would give them an accurate reading of their mileage to the nearest tenth of a mile and also give their average speed—important when you were not allowed to drive over a set speed limit, but as she did so her hand brushed against Adam's, who had leaned forward to do exactly the same thing.

'That's my job,' he said firmly, and set the buttons before she could even protest.

Toni sat back in her seat, not at all pleased by his high-handed tone. She would dearly have liked to tell him just what she thought of him as a navigator—and as a man too, come to that—but she supposed she would just have to let him have a chance to play with his navigational toys as he had provided them, but she would have to keep a close eye on him in case he forgot to re-set them at the start of every stage and they lost track of how far they had covered. It also occurred to her that it would be rather ridiculous to start a fight within the first minute of the rally proper, and even more grotesque to conduct it over an intercom while trying to keep to thirty miles an hour as they were required to by law while travelling over public roads. The absurdity of the thought made her chuckle to herself, but the intercom was very sensitive and Adam picked it up.

'What's the joke?'

Toni changed down to overtake a private car and said blithely, 'You wouldn't understand, Adam dear, you just wouldn't understand at all!'

Once on the motorway system they were allowed to

pick up speed and pulled into the first fuel stop at one of the service areas. There were vans and cars everywhere and Toni had an instant of panic in case she couldn't find her own service van, but then she saw one of the crew standing at the edge of the car park, waving frantically to attract their attention and pointing over to the left, and she thankfully swung over and followed his running figure to pull up just behind the open doors of the van. She got out quickly after glancing at the quartz clock built into the dashboard.

'You've got eight minutes,' she told the crew.

'Any troubles?' one man asked as he began to pour gas into the tank.

Toni shook her head. 'No, it's running beautifully.'

Someone else thrust a steaming mug of coffee in her hands and she took off her helmet and walked up and down to stretch her legs as she drank it. It was nearly two o'clock in the morning and the air was raw-cold after the heat of the car. Glancing upwards, she saw that the sky was very clear, each individual star shining brilliantly as if it had been newly polished especially for tonight. The smell of tobacco smoke drifted to her nostrils and she turned to see that Adam had moved away from the car and the gas to light a cigarette. He also had a mug of coffee and was watching the men as they checked everything within sight. His face was in profile and Toni found herself studying him, really looking at him as she had never done before. There was nothing to learn from the hard, strong line of his face, of course—there never was. She could never tell what he was thinking, feeling. She realised that he puzzled her as no other man had ever done. Usually you could see through them at a glance—and, face it, most men had only one-track minds anyway, where girls were concerned. But Adam was different; he hadn't seemed interested in either her or Carinna sexually, and although she had seen him at work and knew him to be extremely energetic and decisive, yet he was also able to stand aside quietly, to withdraw into himself. Most of the men Toni had met who had been in a similar executive position in business to Adam had carried their dynamism and drive—not to mention a sense of their own importance—into their private lives, but although she didn't like the autocratic way Adam treated her personally, she could never accuse him of being brash and bigheaded. He was an enigma, the kind of man you could imagine might have had a tragedy or something in his past; if you were interested enough in him to start wondering about his past, that was. And Toni wasn't, definitely. Still, he was rather a mystery...

Her thoughts were interrupted suddenly as Adam turned to look straight at her.

'Made up your mind?' he demanded.

'What do you mean?'

'You've been staring at me for the last five minutes. Whatever you've been puzzling over you must surely have worked it out by now.'

Toni flushed; that guess had been too uncannily accurate for her liking. The man must have antennae in the back of his head! Shortly she replied, 'You don't really believe I'd waste my time thinking about you, do you? If you must know, I was thinking about the next stage of the rally.'

But he didn't look in the least bit put out. He merely smiled derisively and said, 'I wonder if you believe all those lies you keep telling?'

A shout from the mechanic choked off anything further he was going to say, and they both ran across to get in the car. As she buckled herself in, Toni shouted to the crewman, 'Have you been in contact with Steve?'

'Yes, he's ahead of you, you'll see him at the start of the next stage. We'll follow behind you in case you break down on the way.'

'Fine. See you!' Toni pulled on her helmet and started the car, regardless of whether Adam was ready to go or not.

The next long leg up the motorway was uneventful, even boring; there was no radio or cassette player in the car they could play to break the monotony, but after a while Adam said, 'Will it annoy you if I switch the map light on for a while?'

Toni shook her head, then remembered that he couldn't see it. 'No,' she answered.

He got out his clip-board and a scrap pad and did some calculations on it. 'We should arrive at the checkpoint in exactly two hours and thirty-eight minutes,' he told her.

'We have to slow down to thirty miles an hour when we leave the motorway,' Toni reminded him rather sneeringly.

'I know, I've taken that into account.'

She didn't answer for a moment, then said coldly, 'As you've got it worked out so accurately, perhaps you can tell me whether I'm going too fast to keep within the average speed?'

'No, you're doing fine—I'd tell you if you weren't,' Adam returned calmly.

'Thank you so much, how terribly kind of you,' Toni said, her voice dripping sarcasm.

'Not at all, that's why I'm here,' he answered politely.

Toni ground her teeth. Insufferable man! Would nothing shake him into losing his cool?

They continued on up the motorway, the only incident enlivening the journey when they saw one of their rivals pulled off on to the hard shoulder with the hood up and smoke pouring from the radiator, the navigator sprinting for the nearest distress phone while the driver poked about in the hot engine trying to find out what had happened.

'Who is it?' Toni asked excitedly. 'Did you get his number?'

'Yes, number twelve. Let's see, that's a Danish entry, I think. Yes, here it is, Eric Andersen. He's in a different class, though.'

'Pity,' Toni said brutally.

Adam's chuckle came through the intercom. 'What a bloodthirsty little thing you are!'

At last they turned off the motorway and headed through the still sleeping villages to the control area where they had their road book marked and where Steve was waiting for them with the other service van. There was a compulsory stop here for two hours' rest which gave the mechanics time to work on the cars and the drivers to grab some sleep. Toni reached into the back for her bag and got out of the car, luxuriously stretching her cramped limbs. Glancing round, she spotted the sign for the ladies' room in the corner of the huge car park set well away from the nearest village and normally used for summer tourists, and headed for it, but behind her someone called her name and she stopped to look back.

Adam came up to her and said, 'Where are you going?'

'Oh, really! Where do you think I'm going after

being stuck in a car for several hours?'

He indicated the bag. 'Are you going to wash in there too?'

'What if I am?' Toni returned belligerently.

But he ignored her question and asked, 'And just where do you intend to sleep?'

'I shall curl up in the car.'

She made to go on, but he blocked her way. 'There's a hotel just down the road that's been thrown open for the rally competitors; why didn't you book a room there? I told you my company would take care of the expenses.'

'It isn't a question of money,' Toni protested. 'It's time that's important. By the time I've got to the hotel, undressed and got to sleep, it will be time to get up again. Much better to stay in your clothes and get in the car to sleep till the last minute.'

'That's just the crazy kind of argument I thought you'd use as soon as I found out you hadn't booked a room at any of the short-stop hotels along the route,' Adam told her grimly. 'Well, you may think you're tough enough to manage on cat-naps between stages, but I don't. Come on, you're coming with me.' He took hold of her arm and turning her round propelled her over to the other side of the car park, and when Toni tried to protest he silenced her by saying, 'Oh, don't worry, I'm not going to take you far away from your precious car. You're going to get the best of both worlds; be on the spot for the start of the next stage *and* get a decent bed to sleep in.'

Mystified, Toni allowed him to lead her along and gave a gasp of surprise as he took her up to a large and very luxurious-looking, American-style motorised trailer which was tucked out of the way in the corner of the car park.

Adam opened the door for her to climb in and began to show her round. 'It has all the conveniences: kitchen, bathroom with shower, and eating area, and two bedrooms.' He indicated one on the left. 'This sleeps four and is for the men to share. And this,' he said, sliding open the door at the right-hand end of the trailer, 'is for you.'

The room ran across the width of the vehicle and was fitted with a double size bed that had already been made up ready for her and looked infinitely comfortable and inviting. There was even a built-in wardrobe and set of drawers, but what most attracted Toni's attention was the sight of one of her own suitcases lying on the bed. Quickly she crossed to open it, but found it completely empty. She turned a puzzled face to Adam, who casually opened the door of the wardrobe. To her amazement she found that it contained some of her own clothes from the apartment: slacks, sweaters and some dresses too. All she had brought with her was a hold-all containing a couple of changes of outer clothes and loads of undies, which she had stowed in Steve's van, as there wasn't room for it in the Escort.

'But I don't understand. How did they get here?'

Adam grinned. 'I got Carinna to pack them. I had an idea that you'd care more about the car than you would for yourself, so I laid this on.'

Toni looked at him uncertainly. It was of course a very thoughtful gesture, and one she ought to have been grateful for, she supposed, but she found an extreme reluctance within herself to have to thank him. Then she remembered that he hadn't said where he was going to sleep.

'And you?' she asked suspiciously. 'Are you going to sleep in the hotel?'

Shaking his head, Adam said, 'No, I'm going to sleep right here and right now.'

Toni's eyes flew wide. *'Right here?'*

He gave a sigh of exasperation. 'In the other bedroom, of course. Where did you think I meant?'

Toni flushed, then said shortly, 'Thanks, but I'd rather sleep in the car.'

'Oh, come now,' said Adam jeeringly as she tried to walk past him, 'you're surely not afraid of sharing a trailer with me?'

'Certainly not!' she snapped back, but spoiled the effect by adding, 'It might give rise to gossip, that's all. After all, there are an awful lot of newspaper and television people covering this race and they'd make a meal of even the vaguest rumour.' Seeing the cold look that came into his eyes, she went on, 'Look, I appreciate your laying this on for me, but it really would be much better if we slept separately.'

Adam grinned ironically. 'I suppose I ought to be flattered that you evidently think me some kind of superman who's capable of taking part in a gruelling rally and having a love affair during two-hour stop-overs at the same time.' His voice changed as he said deliberately, 'But when I make love to a woman I like to take my time about it. However, no matter how little you may care about your own creature comforts, *I* do not intend to sleep in the car for nearly two weeks.'

'I haven't asked you to,' Toni pointed out coldly as she realised that he had, after all, laid all this on for his own benefit, not hers. 'Don't worry, you won't have to put yourself out, I've already said I'll sleep in the car.'

'And what sort of figure do you think I'd cut if I let you do that?'

It had been a long and exhausting day, and all Toni wanted to do was to sleep, somewhere—anywhere! Angry now, she said caustically, 'Quite frankly I couldn't care less what other people think of you. I know what *I* think of you. I made up my mind about you the first day I met you and nothing I've learned about you since has made me change it! On the contrary! Now, will you please get out of my way so that I can leave you to your luxury trailer while I go back to the car.' She glared at him balefully. 'Which is probably what you knew would happen all the time.'

Adam didn't move out of the way, he merely looked down at her with a derisive curl to his lips. 'You know, Toni, you really are getting to be very predictable. I knew you'd react like this—that's why I arranged for a chaperone.'

Toni's mouth dropped again. 'A chaperone?'

'Yes.' He went back to the main door of the trailer and beckoned someone over. A moment later Carinna climbed in and burst into laughter as soon as she saw the look on Toni's face.

'Hi. Surprise, surprise! Didn't I keep the secret well? Adam asked me to come weeks ago, and I nearly let the cat out of the bag a dozen times. Have a good sleep and I'll have some breakfast ready for you both when you wake up. 'Bye!'

And then she was gone again, with Toni still staring after her rather dazedly.

Mockingly, Adam said, 'I take it your sense of propriety is now satisfied?'

Toni nodded, bereft of words.

'Good, then perhaps we can get some sleep. You can

have the bathroom first.' He turned to go but then thought of something. 'And if you get any ideas about saving time by sleeping in your clothes, then I'll come and strip them off you myself. Do you understand?'

Toni gulped, took one look at his threatening face, and fled into the bathroom.

CHAPTER SEVEN

TONI came slowly, reluctantly out of a deep sleep and for a moment couldn't think where she was. Then the pale morning light shining through the window outlined the little room and she came awake with a jerk. Somebody banged on the door again and then Carinna poked her head round.

'Breakfast in five minutes, and Steve said to tell you it looks like snow.'

'Oh, great, that's all we need!'

Quickly she dressed in jeans and a sweater and dabbed on token powder and lipstick. Make-up and the way she looked were the last things she worried about on a rally. But the sleep had done her good, her eyes were bright and alert, needing no mascara or eye-shadow to enhance their natural beauty.

Carinna had set places for four at the table and Adam and Steve were already eating.

'Good morning.'

Both looked up as she came in, their eyes looking her over; Steve's appreciatively, Adam's openly critical.

'You look perky,' Steve remarked. 'Sleep okay?'

'Like a top.' She slid into the seat opposite Adam but addressed Steve. 'Find anything wrong with the car?'

'Nothing serious. 'I've put the racing tires back on—they should be fine for the hill stages today.'

Carinna put a heaped plate of eggs and bacon in

front of her and Toni began to eat hungrily. 'Are you staying with the rally the whole way?' she asked her roommate between mouthfuls.

'Yes.' Carinna joined them at the table. 'I'll travel with the trailer ahead of you to all the compulsory stops and sleep in the room you were using when you're driving.'

'Great.' Toni smiled at her. 'Who knows, we might make a motoring enthusiast out of you yet.'

As soon as they had finished eating, she and Adam shrugged themselves into their outdoor clothes. Watching Adam pull on his ski-suit, Toni remarked. 'You've chosen the best sort of clothing for this weather. A skiing outfit is just right.'

'Why don't you wear one, then?'

'Oh, I've never been skiing, I don't possess one.'

They went outside to find the sky darkly overcast, the grey clouds heavy with snow.

Toni shivered and zipped her parka right up to her neck. 'Brrr! I hope that lot holds off.'

'Excuse me a minute, I have to make a phone call.' Adam strode off towards the group of large trailers and vans that housed all the R.C.C. officials and their battery of equipment, which included several radio phones for the use of competitors. Checking in with his office, Toni surmised rather irritably. Did he really think he was so indispensable that his company wouldn't run without him for a few days? Then she caught herself up—maybe he was indispensable at that.

The driving that day was tough, really tough, a strain on both drivers and cars. There were four stages during the day, the routes leading along narrow roads, little more than lanes, sometimes with a steep drop on one side and often with a very strong wind gusting against them and slowing them down. The snow held off, luckily, but it was bitterly cold and only the most ardent enthusiasts turned out to watch the cars hurtle by. Toni had no difficulty in following the route because she had already travelled this way on her trial run, but Adam had his maps and route card' out all ready as they set off and immediately began to give her instructions, and at the right time too; not so far ahead that she would forget them or at the last minute so she would miss a turning. Toni let him get on with it, waiting for him to slip up and give her the wrong instruction, which she would take great delight in pointing out to him, but to her surprise he kept to the route perfectly, his voice coming through the intercom clearly and confidently every time.

By the third stage she was becoming tired and unconsciously began to rely on his instructions rather than her own memory. And to her further surprise his instructions and her reactions to them began to set up a rhythm that considerably improved the flow of her driving. There are some very fortunate teams of navigators and drivers who work so well together that it leads to incredible smoothness in driving and very fast times, and although Toni had had some good navigators in past rallies, she had never had one with whom she attained that marvellous and longed for smoothness. Incredulously she wondered if that could be beginning to happen now—but with Adam York of all people?

Up until the fourth stage they were holding their position well, but as they were driving between stone-walled sheepfields, a tractor pulled out of a gate ahead of them and Toni had to slam on her brakes. She tooted the horn impatiently, but the tractor driver took his time, giving them a dirty look over his shoulder as he went slowly up the lane.

'Doesn't he know we're in a race?' Adam fumed.

'Oh, he knows all right,' Toni answered. 'But he just doesn't like it. A lot of people don't, you know. They think it's a waste of fuel, or else a noisy nuisance, not to mention being a rich man's sport. And they're right in some ways. But I just wish he'd get out of the way; rallies can be lost by just a few seconds, let alone the minutes he's costing us.'

She honked again and the tractor driver turned to shake his fist at them, but as he did so the vehicle moved a few inches over to the left. Without hesitation, Toni gunned the throttle and shot towards the gap between the tractor and the wall.

Adam's sharp intake of breath was drowned in a nasty scraping sound as the car brushed the wall and then they were through and racing down the road to make up the lost time.

He let out his breath on a long sigh and said unsteadily, 'My God, can you drive! It didn't look as if a bicycle could get through there, let alone a car.'

Cheerfully, she answered, 'It didn't do the paintwork any good, though. Steve will probably give me hell.' A though occurred to her and she added casually, 'Weren't scared, were you?'

Adam laughed. 'I assure you I have every confidence in your ability.'

And Toni didn't know whether to be pleased or sorry.

As they pulled off the road at the end of the fourth stage, she gave a sigh of thankfulness, rubbing her aching shoulders and stretching her stiff neck.

'Tired?' Adam asked her as he gathered up the road book and maps.

'A bit,' she admitted. Glancing across at him, she asked, 'What are you going to do?'

'Work out our position in the race against the official time, make sure they tally.'

Taking off her helmet, Toni studied him for a moment and then asked the question she'd vowed she wouldn't ask. 'You've navigated in rallies before, haven't you?'

Adam, too, had taken off his helmet and she could see his face clearly as he turned to look at her, but his expression was completely enigmatical as he answered, 'I told you that I'd had some experience.'

Impatiently Toni said, 'But there was no trace of your name in the records when he looked you up.'

Adam had started to turn away, but his eyes came quickly back to her. 'He?'

'My ...' Almost she blurted it out, but recovered herself in time. 'Someone I know,' she amended. 'He went through all the British rallying records for the last five years, but you weren't mentioned anywhere.'

Shrugging himself out of his safety harness, Adam said drily, 'If you must check up on me, then try the international records; I've been living in Europe and then America until recently. Who is *he*, by the way— another driver?'

Her mind busily running over all the international names she could think of, Toni answered only abstractedly, 'Who?'

'The man who looked the records up for you.'

'Oh!' She came back to earth with a bump and found Adam watching her intently. Immediately her face froze and she turned away. 'Oh, no, he's just a motoring enthusiast.'

'Anyone I know?'

'No,' she said firmly. 'You don't know him.' Unable to keep the bitterness out of her voice, she added, 'No one knows him—now.' Then determinedly cutting short the question she saw hovering on his lips, she said, 'Let's go and find the service crew, shall we?' and got out of the car.

They found that the delay caused by the tractor had cost them dear, because when Adam had worked out their position, they saw that they had slipped back to eleventh place, the only consolation being that two of the private entries in their class had dropped out, one with gearbox trouble, and the other after having spun off the road and got stuck in a ditch.

After a meal and a few hours' sleep, Toni woke earlier than she need have done to go over the route cards for the first of the secret stages of the race, but she found that Adam already had the job well in hand and he talked her through this unknown section of the route without any hesitation. Toni's reluctant admiration increased. Only somebody really good could do that at such short notice, especially as some of the time it had still been dark.

During the third night they drove across country to reach the starting point for the next day's stages which were taking place on the Yorkshire moors, and as it wasn't part of the competition, Adam was able to take off his helmet and settle himself as comfortably as possible to get some sleep. Toni, too, had taken off her helmet, her hair hanging loose around her shoulders. She glanced across at Adam as she waited at some traffic lights, the street lamps at the intersection mo-

mentarily lighting his features. It occurred to her that
fate worked in very strange ways, throwing together in
this little box of a car two people who were so completely incompatible and yet who were forced to
tolerate one another for the duration of the rally. And
afterwards, what would happen to them? Would they
both just heave a sigh of relief and put as much distance between themselves as possible, never to meet
again? For her own part, never would be much too
soon, of course, but for Adam...? Toni looked at him
with her head slightly tilted to one side, wondering just
what he really thought of her. He looked almost unfamiliar in sleep, his face strangely vulnerable, his eyes
shadowed by the sweep of his eyelashes. But the
strength was still there in the firmness of his jawline
and the angle of his cheekbones. For the hundredth
time she wondered just why he had insisted on coming
with her.

Hastily she engaged the gear lever as she realised
that the lights had already changed without her noticing. As she drove on she decided that, whatever his
reasons, she would never find out unless Adam chose
to tell her; he was so much the master of himself, so
self-controlled, that he would reveal nothing unless he
wanted to. He was as strong-willed and indomitable
as her father in some ways. But in her father it had
become an excess, an obsession that ruled his life,
whereas Adam had all his ambitions—his passions
even—firmly under control. Somehow Toni couldn't
ever see him letting himself be ruled by any emotion,
however intense.

She arrived at the starting point with quite a lot of
time in hand, so pulled over to as quiet a spot as she
could find and parked the car. The caravan had gone

further on to the next rest stop, and the men in the service van had, she knew, gone to stay in a nearby hotel to get a proper sleep, so there was no one to bother them. Toni undid her safety harness, adjusted the back of her seat, and almost immediately fell asleep.

She dreamt that she was at Brands Hatch again, driving her father's racing car and coming up to the hairpin, but she couldn't hold it, no matter how hard she tried. Then it spun out of control and crashed. There was a terrible smell of gas everywhere and she was trapped, she couldn't get out, she couldn't get out! Moaning with terror, she tried to claw at the straps that imprisoned her in the driving seat, but then someone called her name, was shaking her, and she woke suddenly to find Adam looking down at her frowningly. She stared at him, still wide-eyed with fear, her skin burning hot, her breathing short and uneven.

'It's all right,' he said gently, more gently than he had ever spoken to her before. 'You were having a nightmare, but it's all over now.'

Toni gave a long, shuddering sigh and lifted her hand up to her face. 'Oh, no! Not again!' She hadn't spoken aloud, had hardly breathed the words, but Adam heard them all the same.

Sharply he said, 'You've had the same nightmare before?'

At first she didn't answer, then nodded reluctantly without looking at him.

Reaching across, he took her hand away so that he could see her face. 'What's it about?'

Toni went to move her head in a negative gesture and only then realised that he had his arm round her and she was leaning against his shoulder. Hurriedly she tried to sit up and move away, but he wouldn't let her, putting his other arm across and holding her.

'Let me go,' she demanded.

'What's it about, Toni?' he asked again, but more forcibly this time. 'This nightmare that makes you cry out with fear even in your sleep?'

'Mind your own damn business!'

'It's about motor-racing, isn't it? Isn't it?'

His hold on her tightened as she tried to push his arm away. 'No, it isn't! If you must know it's about being cooped up in a car with you. That's enough to give any girl nightmares. Now will you please let me go?'

His eyes glinted down at her, full of something she couldn't fathom. 'All right, I can't force you to trust me, but first, I think it's about time I did this ...' His hand came up to cup her chin, and almost before she realised what he was going to do, Adam's mouth was on hers and he was kissing her.

For a few seconds Toni was too startled to react, but then she made a compulsive, jerking movement to break free. He merely bent her head back and kissed her even harder, his lips bruising hers and forcing them to open, no matter how much she tried to keep them closed. Furiously she tried to pull his hand away, tearing at his skin with her nails, but he seemed not to even notice, his mouth importuning her, demanding a response that she fought not to give. It seemed to Toni suddenly as if this kiss was a battle between them, a culmination of all the fights and rows they had had since the moment they met, and that she had to win, because if she lost... But her mind shied away from that thought. Think positive, never think of losing. It was a maxim that she had had drummed into her ever since she could remember and it held good for this just as much as racing.

She grew rigid in his arms, willing herself to resist, but his lips were moving sensually against her, playing with hers, trying to seduce her as she had tried to seduce him once before. Then she had lost, he had held out against her just as she must hold out against him now. But her resistance only seemed to act as a spur and his kiss became more passionate, filled with an urgent hunger as he sought to dominate her. It was her own body that betrayed her; a wave of sexual desire growing in her like a fire and making her begin to tremble. Frantically now she tried to free herself, her body writhing, her head jerking in a hopeless effort to escape. Deliberately Adam hurt her, his mouth savage and abandoned. Toni made little moaning sounds under his mouth and she began to cry, knowing that she had lost but still desperately trying to hold out. His grip tightened, his fingers bruising her skin, his lips ravaging her mouth. The hot waves of desire consumed her, burst like an explosion in her head. Suddenly she submitted, her mouth opening under his, all the fight gone, and her senses reeled under the shock. She felt as if she was falling, the sensations of sound and sight deserted her and she seemed to be in a whirling vortex of desire and passion. Time was suspended, there was no world outside, nothing but this crying, aching need, and her submission to a sexual domination she had never even begun to imagine could exist.

Her arms slid upwards round his neck without her even realising she had moved, and immediately Adam drew her closer, as he gave an exultant sound of triumph. His mouth left hers now to explore her throat, the curve of her cheek, her eyes, but she gave a whimper of protest and loss, and put her hand in his hair to pull his head round to kiss her again, returning it with an almost frantic desire that could never be satiated by kisses alone. His fingers sought deliberately for the zip of her parka and slid it open, and then his hand was inside her sweater, cupping her breast, exploring, fondling, until Toni moaned with mingled ecstasy and longing, clinging to him and lost to everything but the physical awareness he had wakened in her.

After a while Adam's hand came up to her face again and he said commandingly, 'Look at me, Toni.'

Slowly she opened her eyes, dark with desire, her lips parted sensuously, her whole body still burning with unfulfilled passion.

His grey eyes ran over her face, feature by feature, seeing there the completeness of her surrender. 'So now we know, don't we?' he said softly.

Toni didn't even begin to pretend not to understand. She nodded, suddenly thankful that the battle was over and for the moment not caring about the future. Living only for now, for this space of time in which, for the first time in her life, a man had battered down her sexual defences and forced her to submit to his will. She should have been angry and afraid, but strangely she wasn't. If anything she felt almost humble. Looking into Adam's face, she tried to tell what he was thinking, feeling, but his features were completely inscrutable, even his eyes giving nothing away.

'Adam?' she said questioningly.

He didn't answer, just straightened up and sat back in his seat, moving his arm away. Then he lit a cigarette and rubbed at the misted-up windshield to look out.

'It's light outside,' he observed, then glanced at his watch. 'Steve and the others should be awake now; I'll go and roust them out and see if I can get us some breakfast.' Getting out of the car, he shut the door firmly and walked away without another word.

Toni stared after him, completely bewildered. Why, when he had used such force and passion to master her, had he just walked away without following it up? Okay, here and now definitely wasn't the time and place, but he could at least have said something— anything! Not just left her hanging in mid-air like this. Slowly she straightened her clothes and opened the window a little. Her skin was still hot, her hands shaking. She tried to think, but her thoughts were in a jangled turmoil, her emotions too raw and bruised. Why had he kissed her, why? Because she had tried it on him? Or just to satisfy his own ego, for the pure satisfaction of proving to himself that he could do it? Tremblingly she took her handbag off the parcel shelf and looked at herself in her make-up mirror. Her face was still flushed, but dark-shadowed round the eyes from lack of sleep. She remembered the nightmare and realised that Adam had caught her at her most vulnerable moment, when she had little strength to fight him. Slowly she applied some lipstick and powder and then put the mirror away, torn between fear that he had made a fool of her, and an unbearable yearning for him to kiss her again, but more than that, much, much more than that.

It was some time before he came back, accompanied by Steve and the others. Reluctantly Toni got out of the car and went to meet them, holding her collar up not only to protect her from the cold, but also to hide her face a little; she was afraid it might give too much away. Her eyes flew to Adam, but he was sorting through some letters he had in his hand and glanced at her only briefly, his eyes quite impersonal. Numbly, Toni turned to Steve and said lightly, 'Is that coffee for me?'

'Yes, and I've got you a hot bacon sandwich, too. Not much of a breakfast, I'm afraid, but Carinna has promised us all something special at the next rest stop.'

Toni took the lid off the plastic beaker and thankfully lowered her head to drink it, glad of an excuse not to have to look at any of them.

'You'll have to go carefully today,' Steve warned her. 'One of the R.C.C. officials said there's ice on the roads.' He raised his head to look at the sky. 'And I shouldn't be surprised if we don't get snow before long. Who'd have thought we'd get this weather in November?' he muttered, shaking his head in disbelief. Then he looked at her and grinned. 'We must all be mad—out in the freezing cold all night and driving through snow and ice. And this is supposed to be fun!'

The others laughed at him, but Toni turned away. Fun? How could it be fun when so much depended upon it? And when your navigator tried to seduce you one minute and ignored you the next, she thought viciously.

She got her bag from the car and turned to head for the cloakrooms at the side of the garage forecourt, but as she moved away Adam called out to her. Toni stiffened, hesitated, then turned slowly to face him, her face white and set.

Adam stepped up to her and put a bulky parcel into

her hands. 'A present for you,' he said lightly.

For a moment she gazed at the parcel wordlessly, then slowly lifted her eyes to his. There was a light in them she had never seen before and there was no mockery in the smile he gave her. 'What—what is it?' she asked unsteadily.

'A ski suit. I sent ahead for one. I hope it fits.'

Almost inaudibly she muttered, 'Th-thank you,' then quickly turned and went on her way.

The suit fitted so well that she might have been measured for it and was far more effective in keeping her warm during that day on the bleak, open moors than her parka. By eleven the snow had begun to fall, gusting thickly in the wind and starting to form drifts against the stone walls that edged the road. The conditions started to take their toll of the entries, and although the hill farmers knew the rally was coming through and had moved their flocks out of the vicinity, still a couple of sheep had got loose and caused accidents, so by the end of these stages Toni and Adam had moved up a couple of places, but everyone's times had been slow.

Personally Toni was glad of the snow and treacherous conditions; it meant that she had to concentrate totally on her driving and could ignore the man beside her other than to listen to his incessant instructions over the intercom. It was almost impossible to maintain racing speeds, but the car answered her demands bravely, the tires striving to grip the road, the windshield wipers fighting a losing battle against the heavy flakes that were gusting against it.

Her senses had been at such a high pitch of concentration all day that when she at last got to the trailer in the evening, she found it almost impossible to unwind. A hot shower in the tiny bathroom helped a little, but as she towelled herself Toni noticed her reflection in the mirror and became very still. On her breasts there were small marks where Adam had handled her earlier that day. She stared for a moment, then hurriedly finished drying and pulled on clean clothes, trying not to think about it, to put it out of her mind.

It was warm and crowded in the eating area, because all five of the crewmen were there, waiting their turn to eat, while Adam and Steve were already seated at opposite sides of the table. Toni went to slide into the seat next to Steve, but Carinna turned from the stove and said smilingly, 'Oh, I've put you here next to Adam, Toni,' and put a plate of hot soup in the place set for her. Toni hesitated, but Carinna looked at her expectantly and she slowly moved to the other side and sat down beside Adam. He obligingly moved up a little, but even so he was so broad that their shoulders and arms necessarily touched. Toni was immediately aware of him, as if some kind of electric shock had passed through her, and it was all she could do to hold her spoon steady in her hand.

Carinna was a good cook when she wanted to be, and the lamb casserole she served as the main course looked delicious, but, hungry as she was, Toni just couldn't eat, there seemed to be a constriction in her throat which made it impossible to swallow. The crewmen and Steve did most of the talking, exchanging experiences and surmising on the chances of various other competitors for the rest of the rally, or teasing Carinna by telling her that if the rally didn't kill them her cooking would. Toni sat quietly amid their noisy banter, taking no part in it. Adam, too, ate mostly in silence, only occasionally exchanging a word with one or other of them, but all the time she was searingly aware of the rock-hardness of his shoulder and the warmth of his thigh against hers.

Abruptly Toni put her knife and fork on to her still full plate and stood up. 'Excuse me.' Carefully not looking directly at any of them, she hurried along to her bedroom and leant against the wall, taking deep breaths to try and steady herself.

The door hadn't shut properly and Carinna's voice carried to her distinctly. 'What's the matter with Toni? I'd better go to her.'

But Adam said, 'No, leave her alone. She's very tired, that's all.'

'But she's hardly touched her food. And she looked very pale—perhaps she isn't feeling well.'

'She'll be all right. Just leave her alone and let her sleep.'

There was an authoritativeness in Adam's voice that brooked no argument and Toni wasn't in the least surprised when Carinna capitulated and began to talk to Steve. She closed the door, a spark of anger running through her at Adam's high-handedness in not letting her friend come to her. But then she had to admit that she was in no mood for Carinna's probing questions and would probably have snapped her head off anyway. Slowly she began to get undressed, feeling utterly weary and dejected, but once in bed she found that she couldn't sleep no matter how hard she tried. But she must rest, tonight they were driving across country to the Lake District and tomorrow there were more closed stages when she would have to be fully alert to follow Adam's directions through the unknown terrain.

She tossed and turned on the pillow, trying to force herself to sleep, but it was hopeless. The centrally heated van made her too hot, but when she threw off the duvet she quickly became cold again. Her throat, too, felt hot and dry, so eventually she got up and, wrapping a dressing-gown round herself, quietly opened the door and went into the tiny kitchen. The trailer was silent and deserted, the men having taken Carinna out with them for what was left of the evening. Toni turned on the light and started opening cupboards, looking for a glass and some milk. She found them at last and started to pour out a drink, holding the glass over the sink.

'Are you all right?'

Adam's voice close behind her startled her so much that she dropped the carton of milk and it splashed on her dressing-gown. Angrily she rounded on him. '*Must* you creep up behind me like that? You made me jump out of my skin!' Setting down the glass, she tore off a piece of kitchen paper and began to dab ineffectively at her dressing-gown.

'Here, let me help.'

He moved towards her, but Toni screamed at him. 'Keep away from me, damn you! I don't need anything from you.'

Immediately he became still, a wary look in his eyes, and for the first time Toni noticed that he was wearing only a towelling robe, belted round the waist, his legs bare beneath it. Evidently he didn't bother with pyjamas. For a moment their eyes met, but then she turned hastily away. 'Haven't you got anything better to do than stand here staring at me?' she demanded irritably.

'Couldn't you sleep?'

'I should have thought that was obvious.'

'Why not?'

'How the hell should I know why not? Why can't anyone get to sleep when they want to?'

'Have you got a headache?'

He reached out to put a hand on her forehead, but Toni immediately knocked his arm away. 'Oh, for heaven's sake! First the amateur psychiatrist and now the amateur doctor. Why can't you just stick to your own role that you play so well—that of pompous, autocratic pig?'

Even before she had got the last word out, Adam had caught hold of her arm and jerked her round to face him, his jaw thrust forward and his eyes angry. 'What a rotten loser you are. Or is it that you're deliberately trying to provoke me so that I'll give you what you really want?'

Vainly she tried to free herself. 'There's nothing I want from you, you big creep!'

'No? Not even this?' Roughly he pulled her against him, one hand winding itself in her hair, the other low on her hips, holding her close against him, forcing her to feel the hardness of his body as he kissed her with pitiless brutality. And this time she didn't try to struggle or fight, just stood there and let him do what he wanted until at last he let her go.

She drew a long, shuddering breath and opened her eyes. He was looking down at her intently, waiting for her reaction. 'Why?' she whispered unsteadily. 'Why are you doing this to me?'

His eyes flickered and for a moment a bleak look came into them, then he turned and picked up the glass of milk and put it into her hands. 'Here, drink this and go back to bed,' he said harshly. 'There's only an hour or so left before we have to move on.'

But sleep was even more impossible now and Toni felt physically drained by the time they had driven across to the Lake District. As soon as they arrived at the starting point she got out of the car and went to talk to some of the other competitors, doing the same thing between every stage so that she didn't have to talk to Adam more than was absolutely necessary. The Century Vision crew had caught up with them again here, after following them up the country, so she was able to talk to them, which also helped to fill the gap until it was time to go.

The conditions weren't so bad on this side of the country, but the route led them through rough terrain and through several fords, so deep with running water that they were hardly passable. Once they felt something scrape and tear at the bottom of the car, but the engine still seemed to be running okay, so she kept going without stopping to look. They pushed on with Toni gripping the wheel tightly and staring through the dirty windshield, the wipers almost clogged with mud thrown up by the car in front, trying to anticipate the road ahead. Driving at seventy miles an hour, a distance of about seventy yards is only two seconds in time. Also the road conditions were getting worse every minute, the cars ahead of them churning the loose surface into a sea of mud which threatened to slow them down.

With relief Toni turned into a long, open stretch and put her foot down. Her eyes felt so sore and heavy, she kept having to blink all the time.

'Toni! Wake up!'

Adam's urgent yell in her ear jerked her awake and she saw that they had started to veer off the track.

Adam reached out to grab the steering-wheel, but Toni turned it before he could do so, quickly getting them back on the road.

'I'm all right. I can manage,' she said forcibly into the mike.

'You'd better let me drive if you're tired.'

'I tell you I'm all right!' she shouted at him furiously.

But the momentary lapse had frightened her; she'd never done that before in all the years she'd been driving, no matter how tired she'd been. But no way was she going to let Adam take over the wheel—she'd rather crash first. She realised suddenly that her driving was all she had left; Adam had beaten her in everything else but that. And was now going to start a battle of wits to try and take over from her, to rob her of that too? The thought terrified her and made her more determined than ever to keep alert.

Thankfully the stage ended quite soon and the second service crew were waiting at the control area.

'We hit a rock or something at the back,' Toni told them as she got out. 'You've got twenty-four minutes.'

One of the men shook his head. 'There's a hitch in the next stage, a tree down or something, and there'll be an hour's delay before it starts.'

Toni gave a gasp of relief; it would give her enough time to do what she wanted. Picking up her bag, she began to hurry through the throng of spectators crowding round the cars, past all the service and auxiliary vehicles and the hospitality trailers set up by the big cigarette company that was sponsoring this stage, until she found what she was looking for: a row of taxis waiting for hire.

'How long to the nearest place with a chemist's

shop?' she asked the first driver in line.

He told her it would take less than ten minutes and she thankfully got in and let herself be driven for a change. At the chemist's she bought a large bottle of stimulant tablets and immediately swallowed double the prescribed dose. As an afterthought she also bought a bottle of aspirins which she hoped would help her to sleep. She didn't like it, but she was quite prepared to rely on drugs to get her through the rest of the rally if she had to.

She got back to the car in plenty of time and the mechanic met her with a grin.

'No great harm done,' he told her cheerfully. 'You just broke the exhaust pipe. You were lucky it didn't put you to sleep, though, the fumes must have been seeping into the car from the moment it happened.' Then the poor man stared at her in bewilderment as she suddenly broke into unnatural, almost hysterical laughter.

The next day the rally moved north into Scotland and met bad weather again. Several times they had to dig themselves out of snowdrifts, and here the experience of the Scandinavian teams began to tell and Toni was pushed back into fourteenth place, although she was well ahead of any of the other women drivers. This fact, however, gave her no consolation whatsoever. She was edgy and short-tempered, her nerves at screaming point. And she wasn't helped when Adam went across to the officials' van to collect the mail that seemed to come for him every day, wherever they were, and on his return handed her a telegram. The message inside was terse and to the point. It was also unsigned, but she needed no name to know who it was from. 'YOUR PLACING INTOLERABLE. VITAL YOU

STAY AMONG LEADERS TO ACHIEVE FORMULA CONTRACT.'

'Bad news?'

Toni looked up to find Adam watching her. Screwing up the telegram, she threw it into a nearby litter bin. 'No worse than anything else that's happened on this infernal rally,' she answered bitterly, and walked hastily away from him, head lowered unhappily, her hands thrust into the pockets of her coat. Her father's interference at this stage was all she needed!

Perhaps it was the telegram which acted as a spur, or perhaps only the fact that the weather had eased a little, but the next day they managed to make up a lot of time and finished in fifth place, helped considerably by the fact that three other competitors had fallen by the wayside that day.

Wryly, Adam remarked, 'If this average keeps up we won't have anyone ahead of us by the end of the rally.'

'It's hardly the way I would want to win,' Toni pointed out exacerbatedly.

'I know,' he answered. 'And I'm glad of it.'

Toni turned and looked at him properly for the first time in days. He looked a little paler than she remembered and there was a slightly drawn look about his mouth, but otherwise he showed no signs of the immense strain he was under. But he must be desperately tired, more tired even than she, because whereas Toni could just forget the race and collapse every time they stopped, Adam had to work out their position and check their timing with the officials in case any mistake had been made that would affect them adversely, as well as going through the next day's routes again.

He must have guessed what she was thinking, or else

read signs of fatigue in her own face, because he said gently, 'Only a couple of forest stages tomorrow and then we'll get the compulsory seventeen hours' rest.'

Toni looked away moodily. 'I wish they hadn't put that rest in. I just want to get the whole thing over and done with. It breaks your concentration having a long stop in the middle.'

'Hardly the middle; there'll be less than three days to go then.' Lifting his hand, he gently pushed back a lock of hair from her temple. 'You're doing fine,' he said softly.

Toni began to tremble at his touch and slowly turned her head towards him, her lips brushing the palm of his hand. Unhurriedly he drew her to him and then bent to kiss her—tenderly, undemandingly. And somehow it was better than either of the times he had kissed her before.

A bang against the side of the car made Toni jump away from him guiltily, her face flushed scarlet in case they had been seen, but it was only a spectator who had bumped a bag against the car as he walked by. Nevertheless, it had given her a fright and she avoided Adam as much as possible, giving him only snarling answers whenever he spoke to her and being short and ill-tempered with the rest of the crew and Carinna. They treated her patiently, putting her behaviour down to fatigue and tension, but the realisation that they were being charitable towards her only added to her irritation.

As they had started back south again so had the weather improved, and this, plus the fact that the rally had reached a really exciting stage, brought hundreds more spectators out to line the routes. Toni was getting used to them now, standing near the edges of the roads and tracks and clustered at all the sharper bends, many of them armed with cameras. The media coverage had also increased and they were bothered by local television, radio and press men every time they stopped, but Adam displayed an expertise in dealing with these that Toni had to admire as much as she accepted gratefully—but silently—the protection from them he gave her.

The forest stages were, of course, secret ones and had been marked out by arrows set at the side of the tracks, so Adam had no map reading to do but would help to look out for the markers. They started out early in the morning and so many cars had dropped out now that they only had about twenty minutes to wait before it was their turn. The ground was frozen hard and covered by a thin layer of snow that had fallen in the night, but a hazy sun soon came out and sent misty rays slanting through the branches of the tall forest trees, growing straight and strong towards the sky. It was the kind of place that Toni loved and would have liked to linger in, but soon its quiet peace was shattered by the raucous roar of dozens of car engines.

It was too early and too isolated for there to be many spectators during the first stage, but the second was nearer a town and a main road and as it was the weekend there were lots of people lining the route, which was following an old, deep cart-track only about eight feet wide and set between high banks overshadowed by trees. Their biggest problem was partially buried tree roots, and twice they hit one and the car literally bounced into the air and Adam would have given his head a nasty crack if he hadn't been wearing his safety helmet.

Toni tried to keep her eyes open for them, especially

as she came fast up to a bend; it could be really nasty if she hit one there. For an instant, when Adam's shout of warning first reached her, she thought that he had noticed a tree root, but the next second she saw with shocked horror what he had already seen; the spectators on the inner side of the bend, young boys by the look of them, had pushed forward to get a better view, and one of them had lost his balance and was falling into their path.

There was no time to stop and no room to go round him. In the two seconds she had to think, Toni acted calmly and instinctively, setting the car straight at the bank and putting her foot down so that she drove with only two wheels on the ground and the others three or four feet up the bank. Startled, terrified faces of people on the bank flashed by only a couple of feet away and then the offside wheels lifted above the bank and the Escort, carried forward by its own velocity, rolled over and crashed on to its roof in the track and then bounced back on to its offside, the wheels spinning in the air in the sudden silence.

CHAPTER EIGHT

EVERYTHING that wasn't tied down had been thrown violently forward, and Toni opened her eyes to find herself in a welter of Adam's maps and clipboard as well as several heavier objects from the back of the car.

'Toni, are you all right? Toni, answer me!'

Adam's voice was loud and sharp over the intercom and she could feel his hands going over her, trying to find out if she was hurt.

Her voice came back, raw with agonised fear. 'The boy? Did I hit him?'

'No. I saw him as we went by. You missed him completely.'

'Oh, thank God! Thank God!' Tremblingly she reached up to lift her visor, and only then did the first agonising stab of pain in her right hand hit her. She gave an involuntary, gasping cry, hastily bitten off in case Adam heard it, but several of the spectators had jumped down into the gully by now and had got Adam's door open, and their excited questions drowned out any noise she made.

While they were helping Adam out, Toni had time to look at her hand and through mists of pain saw that the thumb was bent back at a strange angle and she realised that she must have either broken or dislocated it. Scrabbling among the debris she found her gloves and with her left hand took hold of her right and pushed the thumb up into the glove. Knife-thrusts of pain shot up her arm and almost she blacked out, but she set her teeth, beads of sweat pouring down her forehead, and got the hand into the glove properly.

Above her, in the open doorway, Adam's head appeared. 'Here, give me your hand and I'll help you out.'

Toni's face set into a thin grimace that was more pain than humour; right now her hand was the last thing she intended to give him. Undoing her safety harness with her left, she stood up among the debris and poked her head and shoulders through the doorway. Adam was standing on the side of the car that was now the roof and holding a hand out to her expectantly. She gave him her left hand and put just the heel of her right on the edge of the door to give her leverage, although even that pressure made her go weak at the knees. Adam hauled her half out, then gave an exclamation and reached down to put his hands under her shoulders and lifted her out bodily before lowering her to the ground.

Immediately she took a few paces and started walking round the car as if she was examining the damage, but the pain of her injury was so great that for a few minutes she couldn't even focus. Several of the spectators crowded round her and spoke to her, but she didn't hear them or their astonished murmur of 'It's a girl!' that quickly ran through their ranks.

'Well, what do you think?'

Adam's voice in her ears startled her until she realised that she still had her helmet on and was connected to the intercom.

'Er ...' For the first time she really look at the car and felt a sudden wave of appalled horror as she saw that the roof had been pushed in several inches except where the roll-cage had done its job and protected their heads, although one of the bars was badly bent and had only been kept in place by the strength of the rest of the cage. Slowly she lifted her head and stared at Adam. 'If we hadn't had the roll-cage we'd have been killed,' she said hollowly.

For a moment he didn't answer, then he reminded her gently, 'The car, Toni, it's your decision. Shall we try and right it or do we pull out?'

Immediately everything else, even the pain, was forgotten as her brain began to click over again. 'The underneath doesn't look damaged. We'll get some of these people to help us and try to go on.'

'Right. You'd better leave it to me.'

Toni didn't argue. She took off her helmet and climbed up the bank out of the way, leaning against a tree trunk and trying to fight the searing pain. Worriedly she looked at her watch; this was going to play hell with their times, but luckily they were nearly at the end of the stage and then there was the compulsory long stop. Now Toni was more than thankful for it, it would give her time to get her injury sorted out. She wondered if you could drive with a broken thumb. Well, there was a first time for everything and she was about to find out. But how she was going to get it fixed and get through the rest of the rally without Adam finding out was a problem she decided not to think about until she had to.

Two boys in fur-hooded parkas, one several inches taller than the other, came hesitatingly over to her.

'Miss,' the taller one said, 'this is my brother. He wants to tell you he's sorry.'

For a moment she didn't understand, then she realised that it must have been the younger boy who had fallen into the road.

'Oh, it was you, was it?' Anger surged through her

as she remembered how close they had come to being killed, but was instantly gone as she saw the boy's white face and trembling lower lip. He had been even closer to death than they had and it probably wasn't his fault anyhow; boys were always pushing one another and falling around. 'Don't stand so near the edge next time, okay?' Without thinking she lifted her right hand to ruffle his hair and felt an immediate wave of nausea. 'Excuse me.' Hastily she groped her way round to the other side of the tree and clung to it wretchedly as she brought up her breakfast.

When she emerged she saw that two other rally cars were held up behind them and that the men were giving Adam and the spectators a hand. The Escort rolled back on to its wheels with a thud and Toni immediately scrambled down the bank and got into the car beside Adam. The engine started at once and nothing vital seemed to have been damaged, so Toni gunned the accelerator and set off again to the cheers of the crowd, letting Adam sort out the debris around their feet and hoping desperately that he wouldn't notice that she was driving with only one hand doing all the work, the other resting uselessly on the wheel.

Although she knew it was only a short way to the control point, it seemed to her like light years and by the time she arrived she was soaking with perspiration. The television company had booked a room for her in a large hotel complex right next to the control point and all she could think of was of getting there and calling a doctor. She almost fell out of the car the moment it stopped, not even bothering to take the key out of the ignition, and started to run towards the entrance to the hotel, ignoring Adam's startled exclamation behind her. Then someone gave a shout and she was surrounded by people, many of them flashing camera bulbs in her face. They began asking her questions about the crash and she realised that news of it must have travelled ahead of them. Vainly she tried to push her way through, but then Adam was beside her, his broad shoulders clearing a way for her to the hotel foyer, where the pressmen were firmly shut out by the doorman.

The manager hurried across to them. 'Sorry about that, but welcome anyway.' He took hold of Toni's hand to shake it and she collapsed into a heap on the floor.

In her hotel room the doctor finished binding up her hand and Toni looked at him anxiously. 'It will be all right to drive with now, won't it?'

He looked at her over his glasses. 'Will it make any difference if I say it won't?'

Toni smiled slightly and shook her head. 'No, I'm afraid it won't.'

'I thought not. You sports enthusiasts are all the same; not an ounce of sense in your heads! Just keep it strapped up tightly till the rally's over and rest it as much as you can.' He turned to Adam who was leaning against the edge of a chest of drawers, arms folded, his face grim. 'I'll give you some pain-killers for her to take, but make sure she has no more than two at a time.' He put a small bottle in Adam's hand as he showed the doctor to the door.

Toni swung her legs off the bed and said with studied casualness, 'I think I'll get some rest now. See you later.'

Adam had the door shut and was beside her in two strides. 'You'll see me right now! You brainless little idiot! Why the hell didn't you tell me you were hurt?' Without waiting for her to answer, he reached up and caught hold of her shoulders, his face furious. 'You were going to keep it from me even when we got here, weren't you? Weren't you?' he repeated savagely, his fingers biting into her shoulders as he shook her.

Toni stared at him, feeling suddenly frightened. He looked so angry, murderous almost. She had often wondered how he would react if she ever pushed him too far and he lost control of himself, and now she was finding out.

Fear made her shout back at him. 'Yes, I was! Because I knew you'd make a big fuss and have me sent to hospital, so that I'd have had to pull out of the rally.'

His eyes blazed down at her. 'You're darn right I'd have pulled you out! My God, you must have been going through hell when you drove after the crash. And all for what—to get your name in the record books? To have a little fame until next year's rally and a new winner makes you a past tense? Is it worth what you've put yourself through, Toni? Is it?'

She looked away. 'You—you don't understand,' she said unsteadily. 'It—it isn't that at all.'

'No? Then what is it? Just tell me what compelled you to go on even though you knew your thumb could have been broken and not just dislocated,' he demanded with a snarl of derision.

'It—it's none of your business. What I do is my own ... Oh!' She broke off with a startled exclamation as Adam suddenly swung her round and pulled her roughly towards the chest of drawers. 'Stop it! You're hurting me!'

He laughed jeeringly. 'You're tough, you can take it.' Picking up her bag from the top of the chest, he opened it and let the contents tumble out on to the bed, ignoring her cry of protest, then swooped his hand down and picked up the two bottles of pills she'd got from the chemist. 'And these?' he yelled at her. 'Are these none of my business either?'

Toni's face paled and she stammered, 'They're full. I haven't taken any.'

Still holding her by the upper arm, he jerked her towards him and held them under her nose. 'But you had them ready in case you needed them. You wanted to win this rally so much that you were even willing to live on drugs to do it.' His voice became lower but even more menacing. 'And now you're going to tell me why, do you understand? Because no way am I going to let you get back in that car until I know the truth. All of it.'

Toni stared at the bottles in his hand, afraid to look at his face as she tried to work out how much she could tell him without giving everything away. That she would have to give him some sort of explanation was obvious, he was far too angry to be fobbed off. For an instant the memory of the kisses he had given her came back and she wondered if she could use sex to distract him, but one look at his face, set into a harsh frown, dissuaded her; if she tried that it would only make things worse. Swiftly she decided to give him only part of the truth and hope that she could make it convincing enough to be satisfactory.

'All right,' she said reluctantly, 'I'll tell you. But please, I'd like to sit down, I still feel rather giddy.'

To emphasise the point she put her uninjured hand to her head, and after a moment Adam let her go and she sat down on the edge of the bed among the scattered jumble from her handbag. She tried to play for time to think by looking for a handkerchief, but Adam snapped out impatiently, 'I'm waiting.'

'Yes, well, you see ...' She found the hanky and toyed with it nervously, then raised her eyes to him uncertainly. 'You—you won't tell anyone about this, will you?'

Adam leaned towards her, his jaw thrust forward, reminding her suddenly of a bird of prey in his dark ski-suit. 'Just get on with it, Toni.'

Unsteadily she complied. 'I've been promised a contract with a Formula racing team if I win the rally or finish close behind the leader.'

'Formula Ford racing?'

Toni hesitated, then said with true reluctance, 'No. It would be definitely Formula Three, and if I did really well he might put me straight into Formula One racing, the Grand Prix circuit.'

She was watching Adam closely and saw his face tighten. 'He?'

'The owner of the works team.'

His voice was suddenly scathing. 'And just what did you have to promise in return?'

For a puzzled second she didn't understand, but then she flushed scarlet and jumped to her feet. 'It's nothing like that. He happens to be an old friend of—of someone I know.'

Adam looked at her keenly. 'The same someone you got to look through his records about me?'

The question made her wary, but she could see no harm in telling the truth. She nodded. 'Yes, that's right.'

His lips set into a thin line as he took a piece of paper out of his pocket and unfolded it. 'And the same person who sent you this?'

The paper had been creased and he had to smooth it out, and then a surge of mingled rage and fear filled her as Toni saw that it was the telegram her father had sent her. 'Why, you lowdown, spying ... How dare you read something sent to me?' She tried to snatch it from him, but he held her off easily.

'Who is he, Toni? Why is he pressuring you?'

'You pig! Mind your own business.'

His anger flared up to match her own. 'Do you think that you driving when you're injured or high on drugs isn't my business?'

Toni glared at him contemptuously. 'Oh, of course, if you're scared for your own skin ...'

His eyes blazed with sudden savagery and for a moment she thought that he was going to hit her. Instinctively she cringed, but then Adam almost visibly took a hold of himself and said through gritted teeth, 'I want to know who he is and, by God, you're going to tell me.'

Her mouth dry, Toni made a last-ditch try to avert disaster. 'It was from the man who's going to give me the contract, of course,' she lied.

This time he did hit her, just once, with his cupped hand on the side of her face. As a slap it wasn't very hard, but it brought her up short and she stared at him in shocked horror.

'This time tell me the truth,' he commanded harshly.

Toni turned away, her hand going up to her tingling cheek. 'I—I can't,' she said unsteadily.

'Why not?'

'Because I promised I would never—never tell anyone.'

Adam straightened up. 'In that case you leave me no

choice.' He moved towards the door.

Frightened, Toni ran after him and caught his arm. 'Wait! What are you going to do?'

He looked down at her coldly. 'To withdraw our entry from the rally, of course.'

'But you can't do that! I've already told you how important it is to me. Adam, please!'

'So tell me who's behind you.'

She gazed up at him, cornered, then turned away despairingly, pacing up and down the room, afraid to tell him and yet even more afraid of him pulling out of the rally. At length she turned towards him. 'If—if I tell you, will you promise to let us go on?'

'That depends on what you have to tell me,' he answered implacably.

Toni glared at him. 'God, how I hate you!' she said fiercely, then bit her lip and walked away to stare unseeingly out of the window, her arms folded round her, hugging herself as if she was very cold. 'What I'm going to tell you is in the strictest confidence,' she began, then paused and said bitterly, 'not that I expect you to take any notice of that—you're bound to exploit it for your own ends.' When he didn't answer she laughed harshly, then went on, 'Have you ever heard of a man called John Drake?'

Adam stirred behind her. 'The racing driver? He was killed in a crash, wasn't he? Quite some time ago.'

Toni turned round to face him, her eyes filled with bitter sadness. 'No, he wasn't killed. Maybe it would have been better if he had been, because now he's paralysed from the waist down. A cripple in a wheelchair.'

Adam was watching her intently now. 'He was the man who sent you the telegram?'

She nodded. 'Yes.' Her head came up. 'He's my father. My real name is Antonia Wyndham Drake.'

'So why don't you use it?'

Toni blinked and looked away. 'Maybe I will one day—when I've earned it.'

'Earned it?'

'When I'm a good enough driver.'

Adam's eyes widened. 'So that's it! He's using you to pursue the career that he had to give up. He's living through you!'

She swung round to face him, a hot denial on her lips. 'That isn't true! I have to get into Grand Prix racing so that I can dri ...' She stopped hurriedly, but it was too late, Adam pounced immediately.

'Go on. This is becoming even more interesting. You have to get into the Grand Prix circuit so that you can drive ... what?'

Toni shut her lips tightly. 'I'm not going to tell you! Nothing you can do will make me.'

His left eyebrow rose. 'Oh, I shouldn't be too sure of that.' But his eyes were abstracted, a frown of concentration between his brows. Then he clicked his fingers. 'Got it! I heard a rumour on the grapevine some time ago that an ex-racing driver was working on a revolutionary new car, but there was nothing specific; no name for the ex-driver or the person who was going to race it for him.' He looked at Toni and the expression on his face changed completely. 'Dear God, he's preparing you to drive it! A girl. And I suppose only then will he let you reveal that you're his daughter, let you bear his name. That's it, isn't it? Isn't it?' He caught hold of her fiercely, hurting her.

'Yes,' she gasped out, then put her head in her hands as he let her go suddenly and walked away.

'He'll annihilate me when he finds out I told you. When the press and television people start pestering him. He's kept it secret for so long ...' She sat down on the bed, too miserable and dispirited even to cry.

Wrapped up in her own unhappiness, Toni didn't notice that Adam had gone to stand staring out of the window for several minutes until he turned and faced her grimly. 'Don't worry, I'll keep what you've told me to myself—for the time being at least. But I want to know where your father lives.' Adding, on seeing her hesitate, 'And believe me, I shall find out, even if you refuse to tell me.'

Toni looked at the forcefulness in his face and had no doubt that he would. Falteringly she told him.

He nodded grimly. 'You'd better get some sleep. Don't forget to take the pain-killers the doctor gave you.'

Uncertainly she said, 'And—and the rally?'

'We'll go on with it,' he said curtly, then turned and strode out of the room without another word.

It was the last stage on the last day of the rally and excitement was running high. The grounds of the stately home in which the last stages were being held were packed with spectators, sponsorship vehicles, and media men from all over the world who jostled one another to get pictures. There was particular interest in Toni's class because there was only seconds' difference in her times and those of a well-known Scandinavian driver and the race could still go either way.

Toni's emotions were at fever pitch as she stood by the car surrounded by well-wishers as they waited for the last stage to start. She had given an exhilarated interview to the Century film crew, bubbling over with confidence and determination to win, knowing that she only had to finish to be sure of her racing contract. Steve and Carinna were with her, as were all the men of the service crews, all as tense and excited as she was. Only Adam seemed withdrawn, accepting good luck wishes with only a curt nod and taking no part in the general air of nervous anticipation.

Toni looked across at him in anxious bewilderment. He hadn't said another word to her about her father since he had forced her to tell him. After the long compulsory rest he had joined her in the car at the very last moment and when she had been sick with fear that he had changed his mind and wasn't going to put in an appearance so that she would have to withdraw. He had given her no explanation, simply buckled himself into his seat, his face grey and drawn with tiredness as if he hadn't slept at all, and Toni had been too scared to ask him why, then or since. And she had been afraid to contact her father to warn him in case a miracle happened and Adam didn't reveal her story. Then they had started to creep up into the lead, sometimes losing it to her close rival and then regaining it, and she became so engrossed in the rally that everything else had been pushed to the back of her mind.

It was time to go at last, the crowd cheering as each car pulled away. There weren't many left now out of the hundred that had started, and many of those that had survived this far bore signs of the rough handling they had gone through, Toni's Escort being one of the most badly dented from their crash in the forest. Toni let the clutch out and shot away the second the starter gave the signal, driving flat out along the narrow tarmac roads set between high banks of rhododendron bushes and trees that shut out a great deal of the light.

The going wasn't too bad, wet of course, but luckily the weak sunshine had melted any ice on the road and she was able to drive at racing speeds. Once a car in a different class baulked them and rhododendron branches scraped nastily along the side of the car as she pulled almost off the road to overtake it, but most of the time she was able to drive very fast, Adam's calm voice giving her the directions in plenty of time so that there was never any hesitation. As a team now they worked together better than ever before, Toni having complete trust in his ability and responding automatically to his instructions.

As they neared the end of the course, she stole a fleeting glance at their tripmeter and clock and felt a surge of exultation. They were ahead on time. Only a few more minutes and the race would be over. She would be the first woman ever to win a class in the R.C.C. Rally! All thoughts of what that would inevitably lead to she pushed out of her mind, this was as much as she dared to think of at the moment.

'Left at the fork.'

Adam's voice came evenly over the intercom and she swung the wheel over to enter another road that crossed an ornamental bridge and ran on past a lake. The ground here was more open and Toni suddenly realised that there were no spectators, then she remembered that nowhere on the route today had it mentioned a lake.

She gave an anguished cry. 'We're going the wrong way! Oh, no!'

Slamming on the brakes, she began to turn the car, desperately wondering if they could get back on the road in time. Then Adam leaned across and calmly turned off the ignition and took out the key.

'What are you doing? You fool, give me the key!'

Toni lunged across to take it from him, but the straps got in her way. Before she could undo them, Adam pushed his door open and threw the key out into the long grass of the field.

With a sob of pure rage, Toni tore off her straps and ran round the car, going down on her hands and knees in her attempt to find it, sobbing out curses as she scrabbled in the grass.

Behind her Adam got out of the car and took off his helmet, throwing it into the back and then standing with his arms folded, watching her with a grim look on his face.

It was several minutes before she gave up, knowing that it was useless, that they didn't stand a chance now. Kneeling up, she took off her helmet and threw it at him, tears running down her cheeks. 'You louse! You rotten pig!'

Adam came over and bent to pull her to her feet. 'Get up, Toni.'

'Don't you dare touch me!' She began to fight him, trying to claw at him with her nails and kick his legs. 'Damn you, Adam York! You know how much this rally meant to me.'

He caught her arms and twisted them behind her back, pulling them upwards, but still she continued to struggle and kick until she pushed him off balance and they both fell to the ground, rolling and fighting in the wet grass. It couldn't last, of course, Adam was far too strong for her, even as furious as she was, and he deliberately rolled on top of her, pinning her down with his weight. For a while she continued to writhe and buck beneath him, then she collapsed suddenly, all the fight gone out of her.

She stared up at him, still crying, but in despair now. 'Why did you do it? Why?'

'This is why.' He studied her tear-ravaged face for a moment, then bent and kissed her, feeling the wetness of her tears on his cheek.

When at last he lifted his head she lay quietly, eyes closed. Slowly she opened them and looked at him. Reaching up, he used his thumb to wipe away a teardrop.

'I'm not going to let you fry to death in a racing car you can't handle, Toni, not your father's or anyone else's.'

'What—what makes you think I can't handle them?' she asked unsteadily.

'You were stiff with fear the day I pulled you out of the racing car when you stole a ride at Brands Hatch. Oh, you tried to hide it under a show of bravado and you managed to fool everyone else, but not me.' He paused, tracing the outline of her lips with his finger. 'You had begun to matter rather a lot to me by then, you see.'

Her eyes widened as she gazed up at him. 'Adam, I ...'

But he lowered his head to kiss her again, silencing her.

For a few minutes Toni lost herself in his embrace, then she gave a little sob and jerked her head away. 'You're—you're heavy,' she said unsteadily.

Immediately he rolled off and helped her to her feet. Toni walked a few yards away to stand looking out over the lake to the beautiful mansion beyond. 'It doesn't make any difference, you know—you making me lose the rally. I shall still take up Grand Prix racing so that I can drive my father's car. You've only delayed the inevitable.'

Adam came and stood close behind her, putting his hands on her shoulders. 'No, you won't be driving it. I've already told your father so.'

Toni swung round to face him. 'What do you mean?'

'I chartered a helicopter and flew down to see him during the long compulsory stop. I warned him that if he made any further attempts to make you take up Formula racing I'd let the cat out of the bag about his car and his whereabouts.' Drily he added, 'He wasn't very amenable at first, but he eventually saw that he would have to get another driver.'

Toni gazed at him incredulously. 'You—you mean he agreed? I don't have to drive it?'

He shook his head, looking down at her tenderly. 'No, it's all over. There won't be any more nightmares. You can put it all behind you.'

Her knees suddenly felt weak and she swayed towards him, catching hold of his jacket to steady herself. 'Oh, thank God!' She took a long, shuddering breath, feeling as if a great weight had suddenly been lifted from her shoulders. 'Oh, Adam, I was so afraid, so afraid.'

'I know, sweetheart, I know.' He held her against him, gently stroking her hair.

'But—but who will he get to drive it?' She looked up at him worriedly.

He shrugged. 'It shouldn't be too difficult to find someone.' His eyes came down to her face. 'Maybe *I'll* drive it for him.'

'You?' Toni's eyes widened in horror, a stricken look on her face. 'But you can't. You might be killed!'

'So why should you care? You've often said you hate me.'

'You big fool!' Toni grabbed hold of his jacket and began to shake him angrily. 'Of course I don't hate you. And I do care about you. I care about you ...' she stopped suddenly and became very still, gazing up at him, '... very much,' she finished slowly. Then a look of wonder came into her eyes. 'Oh, Adam! Am I—am I in love with you? Is that what this is?'

A look of amusement came into his eyes. 'Well, it's about time! I was beginning to think I'd never make you realise.' His hand came up to cup her chin. 'And I hope so, my darling, I certainly hope so. Because I'm most definitely in love with you.'

On the Saturday after the finish of the rally, the banqueting hall of the large hotel was crowded with people as the prizes were given out and the speeches made. Century Vision had done them proud and all the team and Carinna were there as well as the film crew that had followed them from the beginning, seated together at a large round table near the garden entrance.

Toni looked round at them all with affection, wondering at the change in their appearances that dinner jackets instead of jeans and overalls made. Carinna was sitting next to Steve and was sparkling with happiness —almost as sparkling as the diamond on her left hand that Steve had given her that very evening. It seemed that while she and Adam had been battling their way through the rally, Steve had been quietly and steadily convincing her friend that marriage to a millionaire would be nowhere near as exciting as marriage to a mechanic, and Carinna, after holding out only a little, had happily capitulated.

Toni's eyes travelled round the table and came to Adam, sitting beside her. He felt her eyes on him and turned to smile at her, his hand coming up to cover hers on the table. She turned her hand in his and he held it tightly, his eyes warm, loving, caressing almost.

'And now we have a special prize which the organisers have unanimously voted to award to a very gallant loser,' the director of the Car Club announced. 'To Toni Wyndham, for a fantastic piece of driving in which she saved the life of a spectator.' Adding with a chuckle, 'And heaven knows, we don't have that many spectators that we can afford to lose any!'

Toni looked at the others unbelievingly, but they all grinned encouragement and pushed her to her feet. Her cheeks burning, she walked through a storm of applause to receive a silver brooch from the director. An amateur cameraman had happened to be filming at the time of the incident and it had been networked worldwide, so everyone there knew exactly what had happened. They didn't clap out of politeness but in genuine appreciation.

After the prize-giving there was a dance in the ballroom and Toni happily danced with each of the crew in turn, but then Adam claimed her, and after only a couple of circuits of the room led her out to a glassed-in terrace overlooking the river. It was empty now, lit only by occasional wall lamps that gave dim pools of light with deep shadows in between.

Adam led her to one of the darker parts and put his arm round her waist as they watched the lights of shipping on the river.

'Were you surprised at Steve and Carinna's engagement?' he asked her.

Toni laughed. 'Yes, very. They kept it very dark, didn't they?'

'Mm. And after all I did to try and further Carinna's career so that she wouldn't be too lonely when I took you away from her.'

Toni turned slightly towards him, feeling his arm tighten as he held her closer. 'Is *that* why you did it?'

'Of course.' Then he grinned. 'Although I did hope it might make you jealous.' He kissed the end of her nose lightly. 'Just another step in my campaign to make you fall in love with me.'

'You—you sound as if you were sure right from the start.'

'I was.' He put a finger under her chin and tilted her head to look at him. 'I fell in love with you the first moment I saw you.'

Her hands closed on his and gripped them tightly. 'Did you? Did you really, Adam?' she said huskily.

He didn't smile, sensing that she desperately needed to be reassured. Earnestly he said, 'If you remember, that first time you came to my office with Bill Claydon, I had a phone call while you were there. It was a contact of mine that I'd given the registration number of your car to. He'd used his influence to find out your name and address for me. You see, I was determined even then not to let you go.'

'Oh, Adam!' Her eyes grew misty. 'I thought you were laughing at me all the time on that first day.'

He grinned ruefully. 'No, if anything at myself for falling for a girl who was so obviously anti-man. I wanted to tell you there and then, but I knew it was going to be a long, hard battle. I thought that you'd been hurt by some man in the past and it had made you hard and defensive on the outside. And not only that, but you were so fiercely independent, belligerently ready to fight anyone who tried to take it away from you. But I was determined to break down that wall you'd built round yourself, to make you accept the inevitable and succumb completely.'

She stirred against him. 'Is that what you want?'

'Yes.' His arm tightened, drawing her even closer, and he let her see the yearning hunger in his eyes. 'Oh, my darling, I want you so much!'

A flush of colour came to her cheeks, but she said uncertainly, 'And yet—you once said that you would never make me your mistress?'

He smiled. 'And I meant it. I never intended you for my mistress and I don't now. I want you for my wife, you beautiful little idiot.'

'Oh! You're—you're quite sure?' she said tremblingly, longing to seize this happiness but even now still afraid to accept it.

'I can see there's only one way to convince you.' Adam pulled her hard against him and kissed her passionately, then, when he finally let her go, he said raggedly, 'I've fallen head over heels in love with you a dozen times: the first time I saw you; when you told me to go to hell because you thought I was propositioning you; when I wiped a smudge of oil off your face, and when you cried in the cinema.' He paused to kiss her throat, her eyes. 'I kept falling deeper and deeper in love with you every time I saw you. And I still do. It's like a great tide engulfing me which comes back ever stronger and deeper. I loved you when you were embarrassed and shy because someone asked for your autograph, and I loved you—oh, how I loved you—

when I waited for you after I'd driven off and left you, and you came out of the woods into the sunshine with wild flowers in your hands and in your hair. You looked so lovely then, like a bride. And I loved you so much that I wanted to tell you there and then, but I knew it was too soon, that you had to learn to trust me first, and it took every ounce of strength I possessed not to scare you away.'

Toni raised her hand to touch his cheek, realising for the first time just a little of the restraint he had put on himself for her sake. 'Oh, Adam, and I was so rotten to you!'

He grinned. 'It was worth it—even if I did have to travel all over Britain before I convinced you.'

'Never mind. I won't be going on any more rallies, so ...'

'Oh, no,' he interrupted her quickly, 'I'm not such a male chauvinist as that. I know you love driving and I'm quite willing to let you go on rallying, it's safe enough.' He paused. 'But there's just one condition ...'

Toni smiled, knowing what he was going to say.

'That I'm the only one you take along as your navigator. No way am I going to have you cooped up in a car with another man for days on end.'

She opened her eyes innocently. 'Why, Adam, what could it possibly lead to?'

He grinned. 'This, of course.' And he bent to kiss her.

Toni went into his arms gladly and happily, knowing that even though she had lost the rally, she had won the far greater prize.

What the press says about Harlequin romance fiction...

"When it comes to romantic novels...
Harlequin is the indisputable king."
— *New York Times*

"...exciting escapism, easy reading, interesting
characters and, always, a happy ending....
They are hard to put down."
— *Transcript-Telegram*, Holyoke (Mass.)

"...always...an upbeat, happy ending."
— *San Francisco Chronicle*

"...a work of art."
— *Globe & Mail*, Toronto

"Nothing quite like it has happened since
Gone With the Wind..."
— *Los Angeles Times*

Harlequin understands

Love...

and the way you feel about it...

That's why women all over the world read

Harlequin Romances

Beautiful novels with that special blend
of Harlequin magic...the thrill
of exotic places, the appeal of warmly
human characters, the tenderness
and sparkle of first love.

Enjoy six brand-new novels every month—
contemporary romances about women
like you...for women like you!

Available at your favorite bookstore or through
Harlequin Reader Service

In U.S.A.
MPO Box 707
Niagara Falls,
NY 14302

In Canada
649 Ontario St.
Stratford,
Ontario N5A 6W2

Harlequin Presents...

The books that let you escape into the wonderful world of romance! Trips to exotic places...interesting plots...meeting memorable people... the excitement of love....These are integral parts of Harlequin Presents— the heartwarming novels read by women everywhere.

Many early issues are now available. Choose from this great selection!

Choose from this great selection of exciting Harlequin Presents editions

Relive a great romance...
with Harlequin Presents
Complete and mail this coupon today!

Harlequin Reader Service

In U.S.A.
MPO Box 707
Niagara Falls, N.Y. 14302

In Canada
649 Ontario St.
Stratford, Ontario, N5A 6W2

Please send me the following Harlequin Presents novels. I am enclosing
my check or money order for $1.50 for each novel ordered, plus 59¢ to cover
postage and handling.

☐ 192	☐ 201	☐ 210
☐ 193	☐ 202	☐ 211
☐ 194	☐ 203	☐ 212
☐ 195	☐ 204	☐ 213
☐ 197	☐ 205	☐ 214
☐ 198	☐ 206	☐ 215
☐ 199	☐ 207	☐ 216
☐ 200	☐ 208	☐ 217

Number of novels checked @ $1.50 each = $_____

N.Y. and Ariz. residents add appropriate sales tax. $_____

Postage and handling $_____.59

                      TOTAL $_____

I enclose _____
(Please send check or money order. We cannot be responsible for cash sent
  through the mail.)

Prices subject to change without notice.

NAME _____
                      (Please Print)

ADDRESS _____

CITY _____

STATE/PROV. _____

ZIP/POSTAL CODE _____

Offer expires June 1, 1981.   01256317041